Penguin Books
Whoring Around

Born in Melbourne in 1935, John Bryson studied
law at the University of Melbourne. After practising
for ten years, first as a solicitor and later as a
barrister, he became chairman and managing
director of a Melbourne public company in 1971.
In 1978 he rejoined the Victorian Bar.

John Bryson is the Hon. Secretary of the Australian
Performing Group (the Pram factory) in
Melbourne. He was a member, and then acting
chairman, of the Literature Board of the Australia
Council. Since 1973 his articles and stories have been
published in *Westerly, Meanjin, Tabloid Story,
Bulletin,* the *National Times, Australian Book Review,*
and the *Nation Review.* His story 'The Routine' (in
this collection) was winner of the 1979 Patricia
Hackett Award at the University of Western
Australia.

WHORING AROUND

JOHN BRYSON

PENGUIN BOOKS

Penguin Books Australia Ltd,
487 Maroondah Highway, P.O. Box 257
Ringwood, Victoria, 3134, Australia
Penguin Books Ltd,
Harmondsworth, Middlesex, England
Penguin Books,
625 Madison Avenue, New York, N.Y. 10022, U.S.A.
Penguin Books Canada Ltd,
2801 John Street, Markham, Ontario, Canada
Penguin Books (N.Z.) Ltd,
182-190 Wairau Road, Auckland 10, New Zealand

This selection first published by Penguin Books Australia, 1981
Reprinted 1982

Copyright © John Bryson, 1978, 1979, 1980, 1981

Typeset in Garamond by
The Dova Type Shop, Melbourne, Vic.

Made and printed in Australia by
Hedges & Bell, Maryborough, Victoria

CIP

Bryson, John.
Whoring around.

ISBN 0 14 005906 7

I. Title.

A823'.3

Published with the assistance of the
Literature Board of the Australia Council.

To Morris Lurie

Acknowledgement

Grateful acknowledgement is made to the
magazines in which these stories first appeared:

'The Routine' in *Westerly*, March 1979; 'I Keep
Meeting my Grandfather' in the *Bulletin* Centenary
Issue, January 1980; 'Inventory' in *Meanjin*, March
1980; and, in conjunction with *Tabloid Story*, the
following: 'Children Aren't Supposed to Be Here at
All' in the *National Times*, January 1979; 'Ticket for
Charity' in *Nation Review*, June 1979; 'Blowing It' in
Australian Book Review, November 1980.

Contents

Widows

Charles Rand fell off his yacht, somewhere near the middle of the bay, on one of the first pale blue evenings of autumn. Later, the Coroner would be unable to fix that time more precisely than between six and ten o'clock. Newspapers, reporting that he had sailed off without crew, used terms which pictured Charles as a hardy loner. Anyone who knew him smiled at that.

On that autumn Sunday, after a very late lunch in the clubhouse, he had tiffed with Elizabeth. Over nothing, she would quietly say from the witness stand, I still don't understand it. Charles left the dining-room without another word. The last she saw of him was as his yacht pulled out from the pier.

The yacht was found aground the next morning. It was still under sail, digging a hole in a drying sandbank with the side of its long belly like a disoriented whale trying to get further ashore. An empty chianti bottle rolled in the scuppers. Charles was not found for another week.

Elizabeth Laird was less than half Charles's age. I still call her Elizabeth, although women's magazines and the press more often wrote of her as Lisabet. Charles had always called her that. It was merely a function of his accent, but at the peak of their romance Dorothy Laird corrected anyone firmly who called her daughter Elizabeth.

Dorothy Laird had married a manufacturing hatter in Western

Australia, who believed that his business had begun to founder because of persistent and measurable changes in climate rather than his own drunkenness. When she left him, the marriage had lasted through the birth of their one child and a further thirteen years. She then insisted on the execution of a formal deed of separation. That was an odd demand, since, by then, he could settle on her neither capital nor income. Perhaps the document was intended to serve him with an enduring and resolute portrait of her independence, useful during his tearful bouts of self-pity.

Dorothy Laird searched out the most exclusive girls' school on the west coast and lodged Elizabeth in it. She then financed this by looking after the education of the children of others.

That work took her to wealthy and remote homesteads on the plains. She worked as a governess and tutor. It was not easy. She found that the taste and wit that had made her popular in the city were not taste and wit in the country. Stylish insults in passages she taught from Sheridan and Wilde held no charm for children who sometimes spent days preparing a welcome for a visiting family. Her lessons in mental arithmetic mystified those who, from the back of a fast-moving utility, could accurately count the heads of vast numbers of free-ranging livestock and instantly divide them into multiples of a truckload. And often, after unfashionably early evening meals, she sat silently at the dinner tables of beaming graziers while robust and sunburned young women exercised the delicate songs of her childhood in the headlong rhythms of polo-ponies.

As soon as Elizabeth finished school Dorothy Laird returned to the city. She lodged her petition for divorce. Her solicitors thought it might take a year, so she became the saleswoman for a couturier who dressed the restless daughters of estate and stock brokers. Here, her taste came to be admired.

The progress of her divorce was slow. Her solicitors complained that her husband was seldom long enough at one address for them to complete the processes of service.

When the time for the hearing arrived, she did not take Elizabeth with her. Her husband was not in the courtroom. Her solicitor sat with other lawyers. Everyone else appeared to be sitting alone. All stood, until the Judge had seated himself. He was robed in black, and he dealt with two applications for adjournment more fastidiously and at greater length than seemed necessary. Her petition was next.

The Court Crier called her husband's name. Although it was obvious that he was not there, his name was called twice more. While they waited, the Crier left to repeat the summons outside.

A man shuffled into the courtroom. His face was whiskered and he held, under one arm, a roll of newspapers bound with string. Like one recovering from a confusion, he stood with wonderful purpose. His effort in making it all the way through the door had caused him an instant of indignity he would now ignore. He wore an old infantryman's greatcoat buttoned to the neck. On his head was a dove grey dress-hat of the style worn by British Colonial Governors. The chamber was silent before him.

He raised an imperative arm.

'Place Loneliness In The Dock,' he said.

The duty constable led him away.

Not for a moment, Dorothy Laird now says, did I mistake that derelict for my husband. But the event had shaken her, and she was nervous in the witness-box. Eleven minutes later her marriage was dissolved. From that time, she has spoken of her husband as if he were dead.

The day her Decree was sealed and ready for her to collect, Dorothy Laird was well prepared. As she closed the door, her apartment looked like the storeroom of an auction house. Everything inside was boxed, or hung with a label, and precisely annotated with instructions for its removal. They took a cab. While Elizabeth waited in it, Dorothy Laird pushed through the glass doors to her solicitors' office. When she came out, she held tightly to her breast the document for which she had then waited a total of seven years and a month. They drove on to the airport and their flight to the east.

Elizabeth must have been twenty when the Lairds came to live here.

They took an apartment in a cul de sac by the river. There was a small garden with a white camellia and two pink rose trees, and a patio suitable enough for modest outdoor entertaining. It could not have been expensive. Theirs was one-of-four, had no view of the river, and the entrance was hard to find. Dorothy Laird was not disappointed by that. The address was impeccable.

Houses she thought of as mansions stood on either side. One was owned by a church fund-raising entrepreneur, the other by a retired concert pianist who gave private performances on a white Steinway set into the garden and lighted with spotlamps hidden in the trees.

On the hill behind, grand homes overlooked her roof to the river. Their rooms were many, and some were lit hospitably late into the night. From her patio Mrs Laird could make out the rectangular mesh screens which surround tennis courts and, when the evenings were pleasant, she could hear splashing and laughter from a swimming pool that could not have been more than two happy families away. Strolling the shaded footpaths she pointed out the stateliest of the doorways to Elizabeth. They admired door-knockers made from rubbed oak and carved into the shape of smiling lions, and those twirled into iron pretzels.

By the end of her sixth week, Dorothy Laird had still received no welcome from her neighbours. No invitation to afternoon tea was written to her in perpendicular script with the split downstrokes of a nibbed quill over grained vellum almost imperceptibly arrised with gilt. Nothing was discreetly popped into her mailbox by hand.

By the end of the tenth week, she could recognise eleven of her neighbours by sight and recite their names without stumbling. Three weeks later she felt justified in believing, after certain nodding and smiling in the supermarket was repeated outside the delicatessen, that two of those neighbours now recognised her.

On the one hundred and seventeenth day, by the crosses on her calendar, she was greeted at the end of her street by an elderly lady she associated with a three-storey Victorian house near the top of the hill, who made a U-turn especially to draw the Humber close by her path, drew off a beige crocheted glove, wound down the window, smiled, enquired if she had yet had time to settle in conveniently, hung on the reply, and then asked Dorothy Laird if she would take a job as a domestic, at four dollars an hour, take-home sewing extra.

I met the Lairds five months after they arrived. I was on my way to the funeral of a man I had known since school-days. He had died in a car crash. A newspaper reported that if the impact had not killed him the level of alcohol in his blood might nearly have done so. Like mine, his marriage had crashed earlier, and he too had taken refuge with an elderly relative.

That Saturday was third in a succession of hot and dusty days. I then drove a Bentley from the forties, leaky and short of wind, which I was restoring at weekends. It was dirty and forlorn. Wiper-blades had rubbed in the shape of a pince-nez, and dried runnels below made a caricature of a tearful dowager which would have been unkind on that day.

I pulled into the car-wash. It is a production-line affair. The noise, even in the pedestrian walkway, is cruelly unsafe.

A touch on the arm and I turned. A woman, in her mid-fifties, held up an unlighted cigarette. I lit it. She barely reached to the level of my shoulder. Her hair was dark and tightly curled. The plaid skirt and vest she wore would have felt at home on a country estate. She said something I did not entirely catch.

'. . . day for the races,' she shouted. My suit had thrown her. I wore a dark suit and tie. I shook my head, but she drew me along by the elbow.

A girl in a luminary yellow slacks-suit stood by the exit. Her legs were of the implausible length drawn freehand in fashion magazines. The stilted heels which faked that for her were visible only as she moved. Sunglasses sat on her blond hair in the position of a tiara. Elizabeth's face is so featureless that it is memorable only during an instant of scrutiny. Advertising photographers search to find beauty like that when their product must not be upstaged by any arresting hint of human character.

'Elizabeth,' the woman said, '. . . young man with the Bentley.'

'No . . .' she said (or perhaps it was 'know'), '. . . already: Mrs Richardson,' and she agitated her hand against the air as though there were some mistake here she must rub out.

Her mother turned to me.

'Mrs Richardson? Eltham Street. Edwardian,' she asked.

'Nephew,' I told her.

'Yes,' she said. 'Well. Mustn't keep you.' She began to draw Elizabeth away. 'Say Good-bye, Elizabeth.'

'Good-bye,' said Elizabeth.

My Aunt's later comment was significant only for the name. 'So,' she said, 'you've met the Widow Laird.'

They were at Mrs Raymond Beecham's three weeks later.

Mrs Beecham lives alone in one of six apartments which together make up a labyrinthine building called the Towers. It is remarkable for the fact that the entire estate was once her home. The room in which she now entertains was then merely her entrance hall. That hall, and five small rooms, were excised from others in the building by the bricking up of many archways. Her front doorway is of a size associated with cathedrals. Mrs Beecham is fond of saying that only those of stern will are capable of opening it easily. She then demonstrates by opening it with one hand.

Six paces inside the door is a two-hundred-year old boy. He stands on a pedestal and is nearly ten feet high. The marble face is downcast and expresses the ancient sadness which Florentine sculptors felt over the amoralities of adult human-kind. The statue has outlived its function as a fountain, its plumbing is disconnected, and plants now grow from the bowl beneath it.

A staircase takes up the whole of the opposite wall, and leads to a gallery running the length of the vault above. That stairway is more sumptuous an extravagance than when the mansion was built, and parodies the opulence that made it, for stairs and gallery now give access to a single door. That door is to the bath-room. Few stay late at Mrs Beecham's parties. No journey to the toilet can be made discreetly.

I arrived in time to see the Widow Laird making that journey. She was then climbing the last of those stairs with precision, as if she were only then becoming aware how blatant her bodily needs were to the thirty-five people beneath her. The few silver sequins on her black bodice glittered unexpectedly, as they might from an aerial performer hoping to climb into the dome without distracting the audience from the show on the ground. Mrs Laird did not look down.

Mrs Raymond Beecham left a group, of which Elizabeth was one, and made toward me. From a table beneath the Florentine boy she swept up a glass of her famous and despicable sherry, and put it into the hand which I had held out to her to shake. Mrs Beecham has long reached the age at which the elderly scorn the frail courtesies of the young. She wore, as always, the thin body of a fox about her shoulders.

'I see the Lairds are here,' I said, 'are you helping them out?'

'In,' said Mrs Beecham.

'Pardon?'

'In,' she said. 'Helping them in.'

'Kind of you.'

'Yes,' she said.

The mouth of the fox rose and fell with her sigh. 'The Lairds are starting life all over again,' she said, dropping her gaze, 'as many of us have had to do.' Mr Raymond Beecham had died fifteen years ago.

'I hope you find they fit in well enough,' I told her.

She looked at me abruptly.

'Mrs Laird,' said Mrs Beecham, 'is a woman of considerable value.'

'I had not understood that,' I said. 'I thought they were a little pinched.'

'Not money,' said Mrs Beecham, 'I am not talking about money. Dorothy Laird is the most marvellous player of bridge.'

Bridge has held the passions of many here for decades. Women are feared or despised according to their skill. Some play five times a week. They arrange bridge afternoons which last beyond midnight. After dinner parties, wives encourage their husbands to cognac and port and the suggestion of billiards, so the ladies can play with cards in the lounge. The first items they turn to in newspapers are the Bridge Notes and they write testily to editors if those columns are displaced by the pressure of world news. Large groups book bridge-playing vacations on ocean liners. Most popular are those in the Pacific, since the landfalls are fewest.

Dorothy Laird had been a bridge player since her twenties. She had taken it up to escape the connubial demands of her husband. By the time of her separation from him she was ranked third in western teams sent interstate. While tutoring in the arid homesteads of the plains she taught bridge to the mothers of her pupils, and dealt, bid, and played hands with other women hundreds of miles away, on a four p.m. schedule over the bush radio.

A tournament is held yearly in the Town Hall. Proceeds go to the
Mayor's Charity Appeal. To this event no one is refused. The Widow
Laird waited silently while a rung at the bottom of the competition
ladder was chosen for her. She did not ask for a higher seeding.
A white disc was pinned to her blouse to help her opponents
remember her name.

After the third round she was upgraded and allotted a better
partner. By the fifth she was an object of whispered interest, and by
the eighth she had received nine invitations to card-parties and three
to dinner. She and her partner were eliminated in the penultimate
round, but a member of the losing team from the final was heard to
complain that she would have won had she partnered Dorothy Laird.

My Aunt had never before expressed admiration for the efforts
of any newcomer. 'But that woman,' she said, 'has simply dealt
herself in.'

I saw Elizabeth twice over the next month. At a cocktail-party, she
and the Widow circulated together and left politely early. At the
Hospitals' Ball they arrived together and sat at a table organised by
Elsie Grass and her husband, who are patrons of the Hospital of Our
Lady Immaculate although they are Jewish. Elizabeth accepted few
invitations to dance, and none without first looking at her mother.
I could detect no signal. When Elizabeth rose from the table to visit
the powder room the Widow rose with her. Those actions were
begun so nearly together it was difficult to tell which movement was
the original and which the reflection.

Events then suggest that Dorothy Laird took trouble to assess her
chronicle of achievements, and considered there was still a shortfall.

She now worked, on five mornings a week, in the Historic
Society's bookshop, but the income it gave her was little, and most of
the people she met there were tourists asking the addresses of old
buildings and accepting from her only those pamphlets provided free.
Her own circle of friends was also a ring of admirers – a rare thing
among that group of readily disgruntled ladies – but, evidently, they
were too few. Her ability to dilate that circle further seemed
constricted, and, if she kept a diary of Notes, she may have written
into it: 'There is a tactical problem for the gregarious player in the

limitation of any one game of bridge to four persons.'

That winter, Dorothy Laird founded Progressive Bridge.

Its form is the same today. Perhaps twenty games are played at once, each in a different home. Half of the players progress from one house to another after each round. Entry fees are donated to a charity and the amounts are reported in the social column of Saturday newspapers. It was rapidly popular. And Dorothy Laird's appointments book was suddenly full.

Her problem with Elizabeth was more difficult.

Spaces behind the make-up counters of pharmacies and the rag-time tills of boutiques seemed to be taken up by girls who might have fallen out with their families and were working only to earn fares to Tangier and Athens and Rotterdam (from where they would send home postcards scored so guilelessly with the rhythms and melodies of low-life that reading them sends fathers to stride stiffly into their gardens at night and mothers to toss on their pillows). Company like that, the Widow thought, was not to be encouraged. And, although any one of four owners of art-houses and antique-rooms might have been persuaded to employ Elizabeth on trial, her evaluation of objects of art could count on so few syllables that they seemed more like punctuations of wonder than assemblies of meaning, and deceit could not have lasted long. The Widow registered Elizabeth with a photographic modelling agency, but the woman who interviewed them became annoyed when she was told to exclude from the list of acceptable work swimsuits, under-wear, hose, nightgowns and deodorants. They never heard from her again.

Spring is a faithless season. Family neither to the winter which bore it nor to the summer it will grow to resemble, spring is a discomfort to bookmakers at steeplechase meetings, to anxious mothers of brides unexpectedly entangled in tulle, and to the meticulous actuary of any underwriter insuring charity fetes against the possibility of rain.

In spring, we saw Elizabeth on television. To one hundred and twenty thousand viewers she was attempting to explain the weather.

Weather announcers were, then, meteorologists in university or government service. Their science was one of long standing. The world was as flat as a blackboard. There were four elements: air and water and earth and heat, and the behaviour of each was stolid. The voyages of cloud-carrying fronts were measured in multiples of a nautical mile as if they were ships. Like economists and psychiatrists, failure makes meteorologists more confident, and they were happy to spend part of each forecast explaining why much of the last was wrong, in tutorial tones, as though nature ought to become a more obedient reader of weather maps.

The unpopularity of their forecasting was such that it had become noticeable to engineers of the Electricity Department. For those few minutes of broadcast in every evening, the consumption of electricity in the metropolitan area was so increased by the opening of refrigerator doors, and heating coffee percolators, and light-bulbs in lavatories, that their graphs showed movement of an order that planners of utility services feel justified in calling an aberration. The aberration caused by the weather-shows was the shape of a sun-spot.

Perhaps Elizabeth was one who had never watched those programmes. Clearly, she knew nothing of the forms and traditions of her new craft. The weather was at least as inexplicable to her as it was to the rest of us. Whirlpools of isobars made her head spin. Reading the teleprompter, her mouth fidgeted with distrust. She could not produce the word *meteorological* without a tiny practice first, and uttered *depression* with sadness. Blond wisps of her hair feared high winds and floated even in hot currents from the arc-lamps. The delicacy of her make-up could be sodden by the merest tear of rain.

More than any other human being, Elizabeth seemed to be at the mercy of changes in the behaviour of our atmosphere. Increasingly, we found it difficult not to worry about her. We came to be glad so many of her forecasts were wrong. If a predicted front disappeared, the viewers felt relief. After an unexpected cloudburst, half the city watched the programme simply to see how Elizabeth Laird had come through.

Within three months the programme had doubled its audience. It came to have ratings envied by the producers of drama serials. Maurice Grass was pleased, since he had the majority shareholding in that channel and assumed credit for having recruited Elizabeth. Elsie Grass was pleased, since she privately estimated Dorothy Laird's friendship with her as worth four tricks in any hand.

It was hard to tell how success pleased Elizabeth. If the cameras did not leave her quickly enough at the end of her programme Elizabeth was caught sometimes looking off-camera as if waiting to be told either that she had done well or must do it over again. No one who knew her doubted that the person standing in the wings was the Widow Laird.

Near the beginning of summer, the programme's designers changed the name of the show to *Elizabeth's Weather*, to prevent the confusion of it with weather which could be found anywhere, or, in jargon my Aunt had caught, to consolidate viewer loyalties. The show's success had drawn advertisers of sun-creams, parasols, and rain-wear, and Elizabeth had taken to carrying many of these products prominently with her in the street. Sponsors paid her to appear at popular events. She was photographed and asked to give her forecast for the day at football carnivals and beach-girl finals, and, once, in front of the ballot-boxes at election time.

A manufacturer of sunglasses engaged Elizabeth to present trophies at the Raceway. Motor racing draws more spectators than does our football team. There are more racing cars on this side of the river, a columnist wrote, than drivers capable of taking one beyond the first corner. Some carports are so jammed with machines the shape of intergalactic toboggans that coupes and limousines are parked in the street. In the shopping centre, young men stroll about arcades wearing jackets the blinding colour of aluminium foil, tugging their fingers in and out of string-backed gloves. At parties they drift into serious knots to discuss technical problems which they will later rectify more simply by buying another racer.

Elizabeth had forecast showers for that day, but they had held off for the four hours of the meeting. The press photo I saw was titled: *Weather Girl Wards Off Rain*. In fact, it showed Elizabeth warding off an attempt by the winning driver of the main event to be photographed kissing her. She held the trophy firmly, so it stood with arms akimbo between them. It resembled the torso of a chaperone. The third figure in that photograph was the owner of the winning car. He was Charles Rand.

I knew Charles a little from the sailing club, but he tended to the company of men younger than he was by ten years or more. Most were the sons of families who had grown used to the effortless abundance of things over several generations, and who, if their fancy had run to heraldry, would have emblazoned their banners with yachts, horses, tennis racquets, and steering wheels.

Charles had developed a polite stoop, for he was tall, and his hair was often over his forehead. Years of brushing it back gave the impression he had gradually worn parts of it grey. Although he seemed able only to display the festive expressions of a young and optimistic man, he was, when I first knew of him, close to fifty.

He was born in Hungary, and was later a medical student in Budapest until schools and universities were battened down against the political storms of winter 1956. He had then run, in complicated and discontinuous spurts, through much of western Europe. Within a few years of his arrival in this country, he had built a business, importing surgical prostheses, with such momentum that soon hardly a steel claw, articulated knee or caliper was fitted in any hospital theatre without the imprint of Rand Importers on some discreet part of it. The young enterprise proved so attractive to an American drug company that after his sale to it Charles became, as he called it, an investor in money. Using skills he never quite clearly described, he pushed growing packages of currency across the world as though it were a game-board.

'The balancing of the chances,' he would tell you, lifting his palms. 'It is a serious business.'

He was incapable of seriousness. With friends in the club-house he was noisy. He interrupted the endings of their stories with the beginnings of his own. His slight accent became strong. When he laughed loudly, he turned around attempting to enlarge his audience. At the end of a memorial service for the fallen of three wars he joked about the accuracy of the starter's cannon. And, through the blessing of the fleet, his cheeks bulged with breath as if he could not submerge his mutiny for long.

We stood on the grass and watched the tennis. Elizabeth was at the base-line in a game of women's doubles. Her partner was cutting play off at the net and Elizabeth seemed to be making strokes behind her for practice. Her white lace skirt had been given to her by Mrs Beecham.

The court was the Townleys'. We should all get together, Eliza Townley had said, just to celebrate the first glow of summer, but, by the time Charles Rand had found an afternoon on which he could come, summer was already very bright.

Elizabeth made a pretty stroke. Women near the court applauded until Charles, too, turned and clapped.

'Ladies are so amiable,' Charles laughed, 'when there is, should I call it, romance in the air?'

'What a thing to say,' said Eliza Townley. 'We are amiable all the time. Romance is everywhere.'

'Ha,' said Bert Townley. 'That's good. Everywhere.'

'It is an excitement,' said Charles. 'If Lizabet swims, ladies talk to me about her tan. If we dance, someone will dim the lights.'

'You are not supposed to notice those things,' Eliza Townley said.

'Not talk about it. That's it,' said Bert Townley. 'That's what she means.'

'Romance,' said Charles, 'is not so serious.'

'That's it,' said Bert. 'Keep them all guessing. That's what I did.'

Aunt gave a dinner-party for fifteen. She hired gnarled sterling silverware and hand-painted crockery showing market scenes of eighteenth-century Europe. A firm of caterers promised dishes which would be authentically Hungarian and left them for us, prepared, in the oven. Elizabeth wore a tangerine gown high at the throat, and, where her hair fell across, it made a delicious third colour like the running together of two flavours of ice-cream. My place-card was set six chairs from hers.

Over five courses the ladies nudged conversations about until directions were found which made it clear that Elizabeth and Charles had much in common. Over coffee, Charles turned to Aunt.

'Madam, the food,' he said. 'Memories of home. Pancakes were wonderful. That veal recipe made Esterhazy into a fat man. And the roast is from the forests. Thank you.'

'No,' said Aunt, 'it is Elizabeth we have to thank.'

'Oh,' said Elizabeth.

'I should have guessed about it,' Charles said. He smiled at Elizabeth. 'Of course. Wonderful. The pancakes we called Hortobagy. Veal casserole, Achem. The roast is a dish named for Bandits.' He laughed. 'You know all that? Zsivánpecsenye.'

'I don't think so,' said Elizabeth.

And Elizabeth continued to take us, nightly, through the weather. She saw summer pass, sparkling. Autumn, she said, was a tapestry. Winter was bare.

There had been no engagement. Evidently none was imminent. Charles continued to choose his dates from a pool of attractive women as he had all his adult life.

Aunt took Mrs Beecham into the front room. They sat by the fire. I took them coffee.

'She is making his bachelor days too pleasant,' said Mrs Beecham.

'If that girl wants him,' my Aunt said after I had turned to go, 'she will have to do something.'

A Saturday, mid-morning, I drove Aunt to the mall. She, like the friends she would meet there, would pretend to be busily shopping.

I browsed through the mall alone. It was crowded. Well-fed people like to stand about outside foodshops where smells of coffee and pastries are warm. Conspicuous parking positions are taken by German and Italian sports cars with ski poles across the rear sill. Laughter from the boys who own them is never far away. Husbands in dowdy cardigans and wives who do not know their jewellery is unfashionable find it easy to chat with popular divorcees and widowers in nifty tracksuits who would snub them at any other time. Posies of violet-haired women talk on the way from one arcade to another and do not notice the journey has taken them twenty minutes.

At the newsstand a woman ahead of me bought a television programme with Elizabeth Laird on the cover. The shop-girl pointed to it and said something I could not hear. She then covered her mouth with a hand; the gesture of a known carrier of contagious gossip.

By the time my hair was trimmed by Alf the barber, and I had eaten a croissant while sitting on a crowded bench outside the Austrian bakery, and had swallowed the juice of an orange squeezed in a booth by a chatty girl who kept licking her fingers, I knew what it was that Elizabeth Laird had done.

Aunt sat at the window-table of a coffee-shop called the Cosmopolitan. That shop exists on the trade of people who live within walking distance. When the door is opened gossip billows from it like cigarette smoke. She was alone, but talking with two women at the next table. As I sat down their conversation broke off. My Aunt's face held an expression familiar to me for forty years: Not In Front Of The Boy.

The news had got around fast. Elizabeth Laird was pregnant.

There was no shortage of rumour:

That Elizabeth had spent weekends skiing with Charles Rand while her mother seemed to believe she was staying in the country with friends.

That a gynaecologist who played golf three days a week and held his practice on the other four had fitted Elizabeth Laird with the vaginal diaphragm she demanded, a device unpopular for ten years, and was astounded at the speed with which she could expel the latex disc into the palm of her conjuror's hand as if it were merely the oldest trick in the book.

That Charles had a permanent reservation at a motel restaurant out along the coast road known for the discretion of its cubicles, and where, on those Friday nights, he was known as Mr Charles Gregory.

That Elizabeth had been found by a cabdriver at four one morning outside the locked door of Charles' apartment clad in a cotton bath-towel and able only to mumble tearfully for her mother.

That Elizabeth had suggested, then, a quiet evening alone in Charles' apartment. The two of us at home like any people, as she put it, sending his man and his cook off gratefully early after setting the dinner-table for two at one end. Elizabeth's conversation comes to him in couplets through the open door of the servery while she is preoccupied with arranging this dish and that, and he selects the wines and the music he has chosen to dine with, and notices, perhaps, as she first sits, that her shoulders hold a blush unusual for her white skin. Their wine-glasses meet across the table with a toast worded in a

forgivably selfish way which, for that moment, sets them apart from
the rest of the world. His smile comes easily. The solemn
predictability of it all has begun to amuse him again, her showy
thoughtfulness in the preparation of his courses, the skill she shows
him from lessons she takes at the Cuisine Academy, black roe with
wedges of a mild lime which will not burn his delicate stomach, a
consommé cleansed by repeated passage through layers of crushed
eggshell until it can barely be seen in the bowl, a slice of fowl so
delicately glazed with melon that the time has come to compliment
her: Lisabet, what you have is a flair, you are wonderful, and he
emphasises it, wonderful, for he had once called her his Prize, but the
word had taken him into a corner from which he had escaped only by
using a degree of anger he later thought was uncomfortable. Her eyes
harden a little as she remembers that time, and to draw them away
from it he accepts a dessert of fruit noisettes and cream cheese he
would otherwise have refused, and she, surprisingly, takes more of the
cheese. It's time to increase my intake of calcium, she smiles, but no
scent of it yet reaches him through the heady bouquet of his fine
Bordeaux. He leads her again through the travelogue of fantasies
which have never failed to soften her, and they anticipate pushing
between street vendors in Paris; running across the chilly sandbanks
of the Adriatic in autumn; shouting to each other over the noise of
harvest festivals in Scandinavia; finding a summer hiding in the
Pacific during the winter; next year, perhaps, next year, until they are
woken from it by the crying of his telephone in the hallway, ignoring
it into silence as they have done on other nights they stole together
from her mother. But, as he is about to begin again, she pushes
further away from them the lights of the candelabra so that her face
wavers, and although it is earlier in the evening than he would have
expected, she pours their champagne into one glass which they hold
between them as they have done before when his triumph is about to
be gratified. I have something, she pauses, wonderful to tell you. She
suffers a spasm of inarticulateness he finds charming, and he waits
while she holds a napkin to a small gust in her breath and dries an
edge of her mouth. Go on, he says, beginning to laugh because she
holds his hand as if it were a keepsake, do tell me. And he presses her.
Until he delivers her of the words that freeze the testicles to his groin,

and turn tears of nervy laughter in his eyes to hailstones.

Then he stood. I'll call you a cab, he said.

Charles telephoned her the next week.

'I have arranged everything,' he said, 'it will cost you nothing. Write the address of the clinic.'

'No,' she said. 'Charles. Marry me.' She waited. 'Don't you love me?'

'Lisabet.'

'You never really loved me.'

'Ha. Ha. Mother of God.'

'I'm going to hang up.'

'Don't do that. No hanging up.'

'Then be serious.'

'I am being serious. I promise you. Lisabet. It won't cost you a penny.'

'Marry me.'

'Lisabet. Understand me. I am not good at marrying people.'

'At least do something for the baby.'

'Yes?'

'Mother says, legitimise the baby.'

'I do not understand.'

'Adopt the baby,' she said. 'Give it the Rand name, an inheritance, all that.'

'Lisabet.'

'Yes?'

'Lisabet. I am not good at these responsibilities. Please. Go to the clinic.'

'Not a chance,' she said.

Elizabeth continued to face us on television.

Each time the evening news service ended she appeared, vulnerable and unwise, and untouched yet by those sagas of foolishness and misery which took up the quarter of an hour before her. It was as if war, murder, starvation and greed all happened inside another studio and Elizabeth never got to hear about it.

On camera, instead of hiding her body under a generous cassock,

Elizabeth began to wear dresses fashioned proudly to the curve of her belly and the sweep of her bosom. It was not what we expected. Arclamps picked up unlikely and, perhaps, hopeful tints in her eyes. Her face became softer as we watched. A new gracefulness had begun in her. But it was time, clearly, for the Widow to withdraw Elizabeth from the Weather Show.

They received a letter from Charles' solicitors. He denied, it said, 'paternity of any child Elizabeth Laird may now allege to be carrying' and offered her a weekly gratuity of twenty-five dollars and the costs of the birth.

'This is not what we want,' said the Widow.

She put the letter into her handbag and set off. My Aunt went with her.

The solicitor was a man who must have changed little over the last twenty of his, perhaps, sixty-five years. The lapels of his suit were narrow and flat, and his hair was as short as well-clipped astrakhan. The walls of his office were hung with photographs of race-horses. Dorothy Laird realised that she had not stood on office linoleum for a very long time.

'Ladies,' he said.

The Widow sat close to his desk. She unfolded the letter.

'This is an insult,' she said.

'This,' he said, 'is an insult? Against my advice he makes you this insult. Twenty-two fifty, it should be. But with Catholics, such guilt. So twenty-five dollars. A gratuity, that insult.'

'It is not what we want,' said the Widow.

'Look, Lady. Mrs Laird,' he said, 'my wife plays bridge with you. Sometimes our house. Maisie Ashkenasy. I got daughters too. Let me tell you, in court you wouldn't get so much. Assuming even you won. A celebrated daughter like that, there must be some doubt. Blood tests, questions. Everything. I wouldn't do it, I was you.

'But, let us say, everything is rosy: you win, we lose. I been in these courts forty years. Inflation, I seen. Used to be, paternity, four and sixpence. Now, well. But never an award more than twenty a week. Twenty-two fifty, spectacular.'

'Charles Rand,' the Widow said, 'is to marry my daughter.'

'There is no law in the land makes him do that,' said Mr Ashkenasy.

'Then he is to publicly acknowledge the child as his own.'

Mr Ashkenasy made a shrug.

'Why is he going to do that?' he said. 'There is no acknowledge. Courts do not order acknowledge. Courts order dollars. Twenty-two fifty a week, hospitals extra. Look. Go get yourself a solicitor. Check it out. Then do a good thing for your daughter. Take the money and keep your daughter happy at home.'

He held his hand toward the door.

'Now, please,' he said.

The Widow turned in the doorway.

'You will tell Mr Rand,' she said, 'he is to marry Elizabeth or acknowledge the child. It is to be his heir. He can keep the petty cash.'

'I know. I know.' Mr Ashkenasy was sad for her. 'Later you change your mind, let me know.'

Elizabeth was many months heavy with her pregnancy before we fully understood. Three hundred thousand viewers were to accompany her to the eve of the labour ward unless Charles interceded first.

While she bravely described the changing physiology of the season, passing her fingers gently where the diagram is drawn tightly, here, to show a threat of wind, or there, heavy with moisture, we waited for news. A crazily fast drive down mountain roads from his lodge in the alps. A jet chartered from the Gold Coast.

We watched her lips become thin and nervous. Over two shows in succession she seemed to make it through the final half-minute only with difficulty. When she paused, we drew breath.

'She is in pain,' I said. My Aunt sat forward in her chair.

'How long,' she shouted, 'can that man Rand let this go on.'

Elizabeth lasted, then, less than a further week. The Widow lost her nerve. Five days before the date expected for her confinement, Elizabeth was admitted to the Hospital of Our Lady Immaculate. After four hours of labour she gave birth to a child of three and a quarter kilos. It was a boy.

Strapped to a metal tray, Elizabeth was wheeled out of the theatre.

A nun, leaning forward and trailing white folds from her habit as if surrounded by a gentle and spiritual breeze, steered her along the corridor. Unnoticed, they passed behind the shoulders of awkward young men and pushy older women who lined the glassed panels of the nursery wall. They turned into a room. Two nurses and the nun lifted Elizabeth onto her bed. They straightened the sheets and left.

Only then did the Widow rise from a chair in the corner. Elizabeth looked slowly about the room. She and her mother were alone. She closed her eyes.

I saw Charles, in the small hours of the next morning, at a table in Matilda's Cellar. It is a jazz club that wakes at midnight. He was sharing a wickered bottle of chianti with an American torch singer, laying the bottle over his wrist the way Spaniards drink from a wineskin. There were plenty of glasses on the table. The girl was featured on the programme but was in no condition to sing. Charles wore a silver jacket with *Porsche* written along the sleeve. It was unbuttoned to the waist. His chest was bare. It was old and sweaty.

Newspapers, next day, carried no report of the birth on their general pages but the entry in the Births column was not hard to find. The item took up less than two lines. It was listed under Laird, for an illegitimate is born only to the name of the mother and no newspaper will mention the name of the putative father without his consent. It was bordered, top and bottom, by an amount of white space twice as great as any that surrounded the entries near it:
LAIRD, TO ELIZABETH, A SON
and then the child's christian names, two christian names, carrying the mark of the Widow's own fusillade, pride and insolence together.
A son:
CHARLES GREGORY.

The following autumn, I read, saw more rain than any autumn had seen in a decade, but the claim slipped by without notoriety. Clearly, seasons had come to need the sponsorship of apprehension and hope and amazement to make them memorable. The weather wasn't Elizabeth's any more.

When Elizabeth went out at all she went alone. On those rare days she seemed hurried, edgy, and on a venture which was unavoidable. Glances she drew in the street now turned away from her in disappointment. Her eyes were no longer, it seemed, the true blue of chroma-key, her hair was a tawdry lacework of lacquers, and her smile was extinguished. She dropped her eyes and hurried on.

Bridge no longer followed the Widow. She had once said that charities exist primarily to provide work for the unemployably rich. As if she were a social-worker losing belief in her mission, she hung up her clip-board and her smile, leaving the wealthy to their own resources. Without consulting Mrs Beecham or Elsie Grass or Aunt she asked Maisie Ashkenasy to take over as convenor of the progressive bridge parties, so something, Aunt said, was afoot.

Charles Gregory Laird was christened at St John's, an Anglican church, at a private ceremony not listed on the announcement board by the entrance gate. The Grasses again demonstrated their ecumen by acting as godparents and promising to see the child brought up as a communicating Christian. The boy was then five months old. The Widow later boasted that, throughout, he gazed obediently from Elizabeth's arms with eyes which seemed to them to hold a limitless propensity for wisdom, and with a perfect expression of decorum. Only once did that capacity falter. At the instant of baptism he began to gurgle, as if the seriousness of initiation was momentarily beyond him.

There were no other visitors to the christening. It was rumoured that Charles Rand was invited but had not replied.

Nothing appeared in the press. That the Widow had passed up an evident opportunity to harry Charles further surprised me. It suggested that she had made some radical change in direction which none of us was imaginative enough to fancy.

She notified us of it by mail. The printed invitation carried with it the authority of many others. On a card variegated with the dry browns and ambers of falling leaves, she summoned us to a farewell. The Lairds were going back to the West.

It was held at Mrs Beecham's.

Aunt and I got there around nine that evening. Mrs Beecham had decided it should not become a merry gathering.

'A wake,' she said, 'I can't ask you to enjoy yourselves.'

We took from her our glass thimbles of sherry.

'Do the best you can,' she said. 'It seems like only yesterday . . .'

That remarkable entrance hall was crowded. Clearly, many of these people had never been here before. Most were from the progressive bridge groups; a few from the Weather Show. It was impossible to move about politely. People were careful of each other's cigarettes. Here and there a hand with a sherry glass rose over the level of heads like the claw of a crab and dropped sideways into a hole. Three or four couples shouldered their way along the walls inspecting Mrs Beecham's collection of colonial sketches, and cast on the crowd the unpassionate air of those who attend gallery previews but will have difficulty recalling the name of the artist on the following day.

Elizabeth stood in a corner under the staircase filling glasses from a decanter and passing them out over the crowd. Dorothy Laird elbowed herself about holding a plate of asparagus rolls which she said, in passing, was her aid to circulation. Charles Gregory Laird was in the bedroom and had been, she said, sleeping peacefully in spite of the noise.

That the Lairds were leaving was not a topic popular for conversation. It seemed to be spoken about only where Dorothy Laird was present. Since we treat the future as if it will be heavier with decisive events than is the present, those who have no place in it will not populate our conversations for long.

'I expected better than this,' Mrs Beecham said, without lowering her voice. 'People treat Dorothy as if she has left already. They don't understand what a gap she will leave.'

'It shows who her friends really are,' I said.

'Yes,' she said. 'Really are.'

Maisie Ashkenasy pushed through the crowd. She drew the Widow along behind her.

'Going, going, gone,' Mrs Ashkenasy said.

'She's not gone yet,' said Mrs Beecham.

'No, no, happily not,' said Mrs Ashkenasy, determined to stay bright in the face of a grimness she did not understand. She wore harlequin culottes and her jewellery glittered shrilly.

'I mean that I must go,' she said. 'Thank you. Lovely to pay respects. Tribute to . . .' She pecked the Widow's cheek. 'Much to all of us.'

'I haven't seen your husband yet,' Mrs Laird said.

'No,' said Mrs Ashkenasy, 'he shouldn't come, he says. He told me, say some nice thing to Mrs Laird for me. So, he sends his best.'

She left, and others began to leave. The Widow stood by the door. She kissed and was kissed, promised to write and hoped she would be written to, as, in ones and twos, those easy undertakings absconded through the door in flicks of wrists and lips.

Elizabeth disappeared into the kitchen. She had been gathering glasses onto a tray. Aunt and I joined the diminishing queue.

Old Herb Withers came back inside. The brim of his tweedy hat was wet with rain.

'Don't want to frighten you. Think you have had a prowler.' Withers is president of the Naval and Military Club. He spoke toward Maurice Grass, entrusting his items of intelligence to the senior-ranking male present. 'Along the south wall,' he said. 'Put the headlights on him and he ran off. Well away. Probably won't come back now.' He turned to Mrs Beecham. 'Long time since you thought y'self worthy of a peeper, eh, m'dear? Not to worry. But thought you ought to know.' He closed the tall door behind him.

'Well,' said Mrs Beecham, 'I suppose I should call the police.'

Maurice Grass moved toward the telephone.

'No,' the Widow said. 'Don't do that. Worst thing you can do.' To Mrs Beecham she said: 'I'll stay with you tonight, if you're nervous.' She held one fist in the other, as if she were trying to revive the enthusiasm of a sports team. 'Now that only my very best friends are here I will have my first drink of the night.'

Mrs Beecham poured port for the Grasses, and the rest of us began to pour drinks for ourselves. I remember that Elizabeth came in, then, from the kitchen. She put a tray with coffee onto the table. Perhaps the noise of the door closing behind her covered the sound of another, opening. The Widow's words were not notably loud.

'So,' she said, 'the thief in the night.'

Time does not always run at speed uniform for all of us.

Momentarily, I had the feeling that the Widow had moved into a present which the rest of us had somehow not yet reached. It was the irrevocable promise of malice thrilling in her voice, rather than untimeliness in her words, which made the rest of us look around.

Beneath the Florentine child stood Charles Řand.

'You cannot take the boy away,' he said.

'If you mean to sound like a father then say so,' the Widow said.

He wore a full-length charcoal top-coat turned up at the collar. He was wet. The coat had rumpled about the shoulders. His dress-shoes were dull. He ran a hand through his hair. The Widow was unmoved.

'Say so,' she said.

'You do not understand. My life is not a happy one.' He could not help but smile. Already he was anticipating the incredulity on which the most serious plea of his life would fall.

'I am a lonely man,' he said.

'Say it,' said the Widow.

'Please. You are privileged not to fear loneliness.'

The Widow was silent.

'I have no one,' he said.

'True,' said the Widow.

'You have a daughter.'

'And my daughter, a son,' she said.

I knew, though only my Aunt had seen it, that Dorothy Laird kept a scrap-book in which she pasted press cuttings of Charles. Pieces from two business journals gave evidence for him, if only that he was consistent in what he told to each of them. His birth at Sopron on November twelve 1933, to Gregory Rand (Medical Practitioner) and to a mother who had been named for Maria Therese, gave weight to rumours Mrs Beecham readily repeated that his family had links with a nobility once serving the Hapsburgs. And, that Sopron was so far to the west that it drifted up or down the Danube to political eddies explained the absence of a vowel on the eastern end of the family name. The entries noted briefly his attendance at medical school and his sudden emigration in the middle of it. His present business companies were shown in a diagram, like, Aunt had thought, a

six-in-hand, with the reins drawn tightly to a holding company she
described as resembling his driving-box. The final line of an entry
recorded: no relatives now living.

The bulk of the scrap-book was gummed with newspaper
photographs. Many were of Charles with Elizabeth, but some of the
period afterward when Elizabeth had passed, like a novice, into a
retreat: Charles hosing champagne from a warm magnum into his
trophy after winning the Two-Year-Old's Cup with Line Of
Succession; his arrival at the opening of the revived Gaiety Girl, with
the exquisitely pale model Alessandra, her powdered hand as light as a
moth on his arm; on Centre Court, officiating at a presentation of the
zone final of the Davis Cup with a handshake which stretched far
enough to show the towelling sweat-band he wore especially to keep
his hand dry for the occasion; at Maxim's, seated below a visiting
speaker from the London Beefsteak and Burgundy Club, when he had
clenched his eyelids to a photographer's flash-bulb and so appeared to
be courteously smiling in his sleep; signalling the start of the 27th
Annual Winter Surf Race, sponsored that year by the Pilot Cove
hostelry he had bought in July, holding a Verey pistol high into the air
with both hands, his head hung, as if firing a missile into the heavens
was an act of such hilarious blasphemy that he could do it only with
his laughter averted.

I do not recall ever seeing a photograph of Charles Rand alone.

'Why do you choose tonight to do this?' the Widow asked.

'Would you have opened your door to me at home?'

'You might have tried it,' she said.

Mrs Beecham sat deeply in a chair. Aunt sat on its arm-rest. Elizabeth
still stood by the staircase, one hand in mid-air as if she were forever
about to say something but was confused about what it might be.
Elizabeth's·face shows nothing, hides nothing. It does not subtly
change into another when moments of personal drama require it;
fierceness cannot give it strength or sorrow scar it. It is as though it
were made as a thing of art merely. So little of it clings to the
memory.

'Acknowledge him,' the Widow said.

Charles waved a hand. He laughed.

'How?' he said.

'Before witnesses. There are witnesses here. Say it.'

Charles said nothing.

'Say it,' she said.

'The boy is my son,' he said.

'Now,' she said, 'if you agree to make him your heir, to not less than one half of your estate, meantime maintain him and his mother, we will agree that you should have unlimited legal access to him.'

'Ha ha. You have been talking to lawyers.'

'Will you make him your heir?'

'Yes,' he said, 'I will make him my heir.'

'To half?'

'Yes, half. But not a fraction more. Not a little bit.'

'Money,' she said. 'You will give us the medical costs.'

'Already, I have agreed to it.'

'Maintenance. Two thousand five hundred a year, for the child.'

'For the child? And for who else?' he said.

'Ten thousand a year for Elizabeth.'

'Dollars? You are not playing cards. This is money.'

'And an apartment,' she said.

'An apartment. A penthouse. A mansion. Why not?'

'An apartment here, on the hill,' she said.

'Here. Where else!'

'Nothing less. Do you agree to it?'

'Yes,' said Charles. 'Yes.'

'There is a further thing. Think about this,' said the Widow. 'There are court orders, lawyers, costs, publicity. Everything. A celebrated bachelor like you and there must be some laughter.' She paused. 'Your son grows up to think of you either as a compulsory acquaintance or a voluntary enemy. None of it is necessary. If you marry your Lisabet.'

Charles took a handkerchief from his pocket. He scrubbed his brow and jabbed at his mouth. His smile survived all that but came out of it uneven, and his fist was palsied.

'So now, I may as well,' he said.

He began to move for the door. Elizabeth then spoke, with the weightless melodies she used on the weather show, equally for sunshine, snowfalls, drought or landslides.

'It will be nice seeing you again, Charles,' she said.

Within a month Charles was drowned.

The yacht was found empty, and first reports spoke of him as missing. Patrol boats searched, in precise squares, over the bay, and circled closely about pile-lights and channel buoys. On the third day the search was called off. By the time his body was found, interest in it was considered high enough only for page five of the evening press, where, for the first time, Charles was described as having been engaged to marry Elizabeth Laird.

I was late to the funeral service. It was held at St Aloysius'. The church was once almost destroyed when someone lit a fire inside it. That night was not cold, for it was summer, but it was the first anniversary of the Ulster ambush at Burntollet Bridge. The Catholic community in this parish has always been small, but St Aloysius' was then rebuilt to a scale grander than any Protestant church for many miles around.

Cars were parked closely all the way up the hill from the mall. Inside, St Aloysius' was so crowded that people stood around the walls. Less than a third of the congregation seemed able to make responses in the antiphony. Few, for prayer, deftly eased their trousers at the knee, or lifted the hem of their skirts, and kneeled on the parquetry. Those of us standing about the walls were stiff and conspicuous. I found I was attempting to bow my head from the waist.

On the front pew to the right, I can see Elsie and Maurice Grass sitting with Elizabeth and Dorothy Laird. Elizabeth wears a filigree black mantilla which barely darkens the colour of her hair but hides her face. It will also hide an incompatible expression of composure. She holds Charles Gregory Laird in her arms. Dorothy Laird is crouched shakily forward. Few who watch her have any doubt that she is deeply afflicted with grief.

On the opposite side of the aisle is Mrs Raymond Beecham, who has attended no funeral since that of her husband. She sits next to my

Aunt. Both wear one glove and clutch the other. Then Mrs
Ashkenasy, whose attempts at the forms and responses is brighter
than those of the other two, but not nearly so good as the Grasses.
Her husband is not here. Mrs Ashkenasy has already told Dorothy
Laird that Charles left no Will.

Other pews through the church seem to be filled in groups. Ladies
are here for Dorothy Laird, in more hats today than her husband
would have produced in a month. Five dark suits near the front
might be businessmen somehow close to Charles' enterprises, for there
are no wives with them. Classily dressed young men whose girlfriends
have covered their hair with printed scarves are drivers of fast motor-
cars. Behind them are owners of horses who will be appraising already
the value and potential of bloodstock in the Rand stable, and the
buffs from lawn tennis, lobbying for the vacant chair at the
committee-table, and, more anonymously, secretly tearful women who
will now blame Elizabeth bitterly for every romantic misfortune that
happens to them during the rest of their lives.

Charles Gregory Laird has behaved well throughout, sounding his
delight and admiration only at the showiest cascades from the organ.
He is yet unperturbed by his illegitimacy. He is unperturbed by the
fact that his mother is not his father's widow and will inherit
nothing, and that his grandmother is as penniless as she ever was. He
is unworried that he is half-orphaned before he has seen the end of his
first year, although it might suit the sombre colours of his
adolescence to then become soulful about it. He will not inherit, as
was promised him, one half of his father's estate. He will inherit it all.

Although he will not be able to exercise over it the whims of
suzerainty for more than another twenty years, Charles Gregory Laird
has joined those ranks which his grandmother was fond of calling the
unemployably wealthy.

The service is closing. The Priest treads the aisle slowly to the
doors of the church. He swings a censer ceaselessly from one side of
his holy path to the other. The hymn he sings is in a Latin now loved
only by clergy and the rote teachers of High Anglican schoolboys.
Few of those for whom the words are sung can understand it. But it is
a psalm known also in English. Out of the depths have I cried to
thee, O Lord; Lord hear my voice. The censer gives out a purple

incense. Its vapours were thought useful in dispelling faintness in the devoted and in warding off artifices of the devil. Forgive me, Father, but no one seems to take this literally any more, yet it is given, and we receive it, as if every sign and character is fundamental to our existence. The Priest's face is solemn. He is followed by a procession of acolytes, altar-boys and choir-boys in song, and, although their heads roll to the tolling of bells, their footsteps are pious and certain. The mouth of even the smallest is grave. Again I am struck by the capacity of some for great feats of seriousness.

That capacity will not be part of the Rand inheritance. I do not believe that Charles, sober or drunk, had it, even on the pale blue evening he lost his footing and fell off his yacht into the water.

I can picture it clearly.

He falls deeply and, as one does in a dream, into a miraculous surge of comfort.

His astonishment seems to him inexplicably noiseless. The silence is so profound that his lips are incapable against it. The mean aftertaste of his chianti is suddenly full and salty on the tongue.

His memory has already misplaced the order of things, for only now an instant of vertigo passes through him. It briefly blurs his vision. He blinks away an absurd suspicion that it is a dryness which stings in the corners of his eyes. There is no point, he remembers from somewhere, in struggling blindly, but it is reasonable, from where he is, to struggle in full view of himself. He waves his hands and his legs. They mime the actions of a clowning swimmer, God, I am being serious, and give him no sensation of leverage. He seems merely to have rolled over like the four blades of a disabled windmill. The concept of direction itself seems no longer to be logical.

For the first time, he associates a stiffening in his chest with the threat of fatigue. The carillon he hears has something to do, he knows, with pressure in his ears. He draws up his knees, and squints for a more meticulous view of the bubbles which trickle like bright grains of sand from seams in the legs of his shorts. His pockets are heavy. They bump ponderously, like wads of sanctified coins used to swell the pockets of departed paupers so they are not buried penniless at funerals where boys of the parish are made to swell the numbers of the procession, so they turn their faces to each other, furtively, to show caricatures of ludicrous piety, and in those cryptic instants indelibly infect themselves with the delicious and terrifying threat of merriment at irrepressibly solemn moments. He now strains against the grimace which only children think of as a useful suppression of frivolity, and, while his pockets pull in opposite directions and he grasps one with each hand as if trying to unweight them, and while the bubbles expressing from his shorts become so confused about their proper path to the surface that they stream along his thighs to sink away impossibly heavily toward the floor of the sea, he tightens his throat to postpone the time he must open his mouth and begin to laugh.

Children Aren't Supposed
to Be Here at All

Our apartment has the best view in Sydney.

Father tells us often. A panorama wall-to-wall. Two hundred feet above the harbour, and every foot a thousand dollars. How much is that in metres, Troilus asked and walked away before his father could think of it. Troilus is six.

We look out over our pier. It stands on piles, a path over the water, whitewashed thumbs for holding Owners' Craft Only from washing away with the tide. Troilus thinks we should have a boat. A boat, his father said, is a risk, how do you realise an investment that is sunk? Troilus crooked his finger into a boat-hook, you fish it up again. Boats, father sucked his teeth dry, boats will not hold their value.

Troilus squinted through his windscreen, twenty-two storeys high. There is no salt on it.

My parents' friends visit the Apartment most nights. The living-room fills with stories above the music, the brushing together of autumn mohair from Scandinavia, we're all into texture this year, lacquered fingernails wave away the smoke. Mother keeps the drapes open to air the view.

She likes us to mix around before we go to bed. It's not so bad for me, I'm twelve, but it's an effort for Troilus. He sleeps in the next morning. Particularly, he doesn't like meeting their new friends. Neither do I. Introduce yourselves now, and my mother moves off

31

swirling her caftan to drink with another group, purposefully not looking back. Hullo, this is my brother Troilus and I am Cassandra. If they are trying not to laugh, I laugh first and then they're sorry about that. It works OK.

Troilus hates to be made to stay too long. He will say a few unconnected things to confuse them, and after a short silence or two we can go. Troilus, you will get us both into trouble.

It's a rule of the household, individually for everyone, so we all have separate rooms. My father is an architect and into real estate now, he is keen on individuality. And that's why I am so successful, success is getting what you set out to get, my father explains it to Troilus. They explain all the longer words, it's a rule of the household, we don't talk down to the children.

For the last month, Troilus has been going to bed early. He says he reads a lot. I doubt that, but couldn't begin to guess what he does. He sings late at night. A pale sound, thin as the first strands of mist. I can never catch the tune.

The Apartment takes the whole of the twenty-second floor. Above us is the roofgarden, and swaying potted shrubs crisp on one side, and a ruffled blue pool. My father told me the pool is on the roof because it gets the sun. That sounded all right to me, I had asked the question. But Troilus pulled his jacket tightly closed. That's stupid, it's too windy. His father answered him slowly, you can't have everything. What have we got, Troilus said, if we can't use it?

We are allowed onto the roofgarden, but only with someone. Mother is afraid we might climb about and fall off. People fall off tall buildings, she said as we looked down. I asked how many. She didn't understand. How many people in the one year fall off tall buildings in Sydney? She leaned over the concrete rampart and did not answer immediately. Wearing a pale blue slacksuit made for her by Fiorucci in Milan, her legs looked very long, though her knees are beginning to turn in. I know she thinks her legs are her best feature. She used to be a top model, a super-thin. The wind was blowing her hair untidy, a thing she hates, I could see grey seeping up the roots. I don't know exactly, she said, dozens. The cars in the lot looked smaller than in a dream.

Then some people must mean to fall off, Troilus shouted suddenly next to her, the ends of his words whipped away with the wind, he was so far over. She took us downstairs. Mother is right, I don't know what we can do with him, either.

You are going to be a looker too, my mother will tell me, if you care for your complexion and keep brushing your hair. Yes, I do. You can be a top earner, she will say, I was a top earner. Mother owns a small model agency, she will laugh, not for small models. She is, she laughs, too far past her prime to get work herself, her hand angled onto the bump of her hip. She has photographs pinned to the walls of her en suite she calls it, her dressingroom, Troilus. From *Harpers & Queen*, *Vogue*, circulations in the hundreds of thousands, father will tell us. Fifty shots to one print for some of them. Photographers just burn film if they like you, she will say, and I will go into the routine, headup, click, chin to shoulder, click, hands to knee, click, pout, click. Good, she will say, very good, you'll make it OK, look after your complexion, yes I do mother, and she will sit slack on her regency stool gazing into the gilded mirror while I am silent. She has a way of opening her mouth instead of smiling that does not crack her make-up. I can do that already but I don't tell her.

Troilus never goes into her dressingroom. He likes her best, he says, when she first gets up in the morning.

He will not kiss her when she arrives home at night. She is never later than six, but her face is brittle and she still smells of a heavy lunch and perfumed gin from the crystal decanter in the dining-room. She is slow, and irritable if we are loud, I'm sorry I'm just tired, and she orders our dinner from the restaurant on the ground floor. Father doesn't like her doing that, it costs a fortune, iniquitous. He sent us to the TV room while they talked about that again. I turned the TV up, over the faltering gusts of their voices, but Troilus leaned his head against the door and I could not pull him away. What are latch-key children? I don't know, I've never seen one. We were quiet until we could go to bed.

The Apartment is on strata title, my father will tell new friends but never before the third drink, and cost the mint. But it's a hedge against inflation, good property is never a bad buy, prime position yields a prime return, if he is forced to sell. To sell, Troilus hates to hear him say it. The threat buffets his face and his eyes sting. I have seen that.

Don't you like living with us? Father made himself incredulous. He waited for Troilus to answer. Yes, softly. Troilus had made a periscope to look into the apartment below. An empty wine-box, the best bulk red in the Hunter Valley, my father met the vintner, and a mirror, and a long string. We just lower it down and see what's there. He sat side-saddle on the windowsill. The wind took the box like a kite, out and up, until the yards of hanging string began to belly, and the box dropped. Troilus leaned out reefing in the slack hand over hand, frantic as a fisherman. The line tightened. It pulled into his fingers like gut. I caught Troilus by the sweater and tumbled him back into the room. There was an explosion from below. I looked over the sill. Shattered glass sparkled like sleet in the wind.

Troilus's face was the grey of watching himself fall.

Father made him stand up. You don't want to live with someone else? His mother was in her bedroom. No, I like it here, please. It was patently a lie, but inevitable. Father sucked his teeth dry, children aren't supposed to be here at all, you know that. We did both know that, but it didn't seem so serious before. No children, no pets. Father was inexorable, if it doesn't work out we will have to sell up. Troilus sucked his knuckles white, what will this desirable four bedroom family bring on the open market, he could hear it, the only true value is market value. Troilus didn't say anything. It wasn't my fault, I said, and turned away.

Father noticed the balcony had become a colony for early morning gulls, bobbing along the parapet, pearly grey heads glaring through the glass one red eye at a time. Father scraped away from the breakfast table, and fluttered them off, waving his arms overhead with the distress of a signalling survivor. Pets are not allowed, if we encourage those birds they could be construed to be our pets in a court of law, constructive ownership, he said, and they dirty the balcony with their business. Troilus poked at the crusts on the side of his plate, they've got to shit somewhere, he said, and father made him leave the table.

Troilus made straight for his room after school every day. He had his dinner there. I heard him singing at night.

Father left on a hunting trip by light aircraft to shoot camels and brumbies in the Northern Territory. He had bought a rifle especially, feel the action, two walnut stocks carved by the craftsmen of Munich to the Aga Khan's personal specification, two, this is the other one, a steal. Father stacked his gear into the lift, rucksack with a super-lite frame, saffron silk hiking tent, Katmandu sleepingbag with hood. The rifle was slung over his shoulder. He waved.

You could, Troilus shouted but only as the doors were closing, ride them out to shoot the camels and kill the horses afterwards. Mother pulled him away.

We had a party here the next night. It was catered by the restaurant on the ground floor. Mother was still dancing with Mister Broderick when I got up, I didn't know he could dance. The room smelled of cigarette butts and spilled claret. They danced very slowly, as if they were asleep together. He is my father's friend and in real estate, he often laughs, I wouldn't let my best friend beat me to any deal. They were surprised it was morning. He said again I was going to be as pretty as mother, stroking my hair.

Troilus was up late and went straight to school.

Walking home, he wouldn't talk and I was irritated with him, he was drawing out his hurt, sucking the white bones of his knuckles. Mother won't let him suck his thumb. I lifted Troilus up, he pushed the main-door buzzer, and through the speaker said who it was, the door clicked and we pushed it open. If this is such a great area, Troilus said, I don't know why we take all this care. Old Gyngell mumbled into the foyer still pulling on his blue coat, and turned the lift key. Again Troilus went to his room.

Facing across the harbour, I brushed my hair, I do, mother, curls tumbling over my chest, good, very Sassoon, make it bounce.

Troilus sat down beside me, gentle, and though he had not been alone long, had the softness of half-sleep about him. We gazed through the glass wall, the harbour a warm blue, three ships dark at the naval dock, chunky green ferries, a yacht ballooning a yellow sunburst with opals in its wake, and the city stacked around it tall as new columns in a fallen wall. The best view in Sydney, panorama wall-to-wall, a thousand dollars a foot.

All that view, Troilus said, locks us in.

A quick noise behind us, as sudden as the wings of a fast bird. The sound flutters from a redwood panel built around the air-conditioner. The noise changes, to the turn-table sound of a pick-up scraping a record, to a sharp grinding of tin. It stops. No longer a slithering of air from the ducting. The apartment is silent.

The air-conditioner, it's stuck. Troilus does not move. Turn it off, he whispers. No need, it's done that itself. His eyes narrow to the pupils, turn it off, now. I climb onto the bench to reach the thermostat. It's silly to get upset, it couldn't be our fault. Two switches click to off, one is marked Fan. The fan, I tell him, and climb down. Troilus is not in the room at all.

I don't know why something is so wrong. Troilus. They will know it is not our fault, I call a little higher, walking toward his bedroom, feet slapping cold on the tiles.

The side of Troilus's room is against the wall of the air-conditioner. I call, you can't fix it from there. Troilus is a tinkerer, god knows why she says, your father does nothing at home, and toys are to stay in your room or I'll throw them out. Parts of his grandfather's crystal wireless-set he called it, the speedometer from a 1940 Buick swapped at school for a postcard mother sent him of New York but he never told her, not much but everything a prize, a cardboard box he had wound around with shining wire and mother caught him jamming it into the electricity outlet, it's a radiator, he said, I'm cold.

Troilus has his back to me. His legs and elbows are smudged the lavender grey of old dust, the air-conditioning duct is an empty square in the skirtingboard, the grate lies face down on the floor. You couldn't believe he'd got in there it's so small.

Troilus, I say and softly. His face is tiny, his eyes squeeze tightly closed, left cheek freckled, a dark red soaks across the front of his velour sweater, mother will kill us.

He is holding a cat.

His fingers are wet gloves with its blood. It's not my fault, he says, I didn't know she would. I can see the edge of a saucer inside the duct.

The cat is not moving. Let me see please. Troilus half turns away. He makes his mouth work, she's hurt. His eyes are mirrors. The cat's head is shapeless where the ginger fur has clotted and the brown nose tilts like a suede button. It's hurt all right.

Troilus blinks to clear his eyes. Get the cat ambulance, he whispers.

There's no cat ambulance I tell him, and reach for the cat. Get the cat ambulance, and he squeezes the cat with his effort. I have never heard him scream in the Apartment before. The room shimmers with his words after his mouth has closed.

The telephone book is under a phone in the study. There is no cat ambulance. I get it under Pet. Hampton Park Pet Hospital and Ambulance Service, Give Your Pet The Royal Treatment. She takes my name and address before she will listen. What authority do you have, and I tell her it is an emergency. She doesn't answer, I tell her Bankcard. We don't take dead animals, but I don't understand what she means. Is it breathing she asks, and I tell Troilus they don't take animals that, who, are dead and not breathing.

She's breathing, she's breathing, and he squeezes the cat to his chest so it's throat honks like a duck, and I say you can hear that, it's breathing, and she sends one in a minute.

We are down into the foyer and old Gyngell is pulling on his coat. He looks at the cat and puts a thin hand down to Troilus's shoulder. I tell old Gyngell about the pet ambulance and we wait inside the sliding doors and watch the driveway. He doesn't ask more about the cat. Troilus's head is leaning on the bone of his old thigh. Animals aren't supposed to be here at all, I say.

Old Gyngell doesn't answer that for a minute. He and Troilus are looking at me. There is no expression on their faces at all. A white van pulls up in the drive, and old Gyngell opens the sliding doors. Say she is your parents' cat, I catch as I pass him.

The driver is breezy, in white overalls and a hand painted cream tie. He looks at the cat but does not move to take it. His moustache runs down the sides of his chin. I remember my mother's younger brother who stroked his moustache with his fingers a lot and sold used sports cars from home on weekends. He's dead now.

The driver hands me a clip-board and ball-pen. Sign for the ambulance, and he takes a white towel from inside the rear door. He drapes it over his hands so that only their shapes show through. Here, he says to Troilus, I'll see if it's alive. Troilus drops his head to the cat. It's breathing, he whispers.

The cat is panting. Its eyes are still closed, the fur tufted over them, but its mouth is open, the tiny tongue a pink camellia petal fluttering in its breath.

Oxygen, he takes the clip-board and makes a mark, sign here. As I sign, Troilus says yes, it's a very good cat, sign for oxygen.

Three in the front, the van has a hard ride. The driver wheels it fast between the traffic. I think of the cat in a hissing perspex box in the back, the sides of the box clear as oxygen. The driver turns the radio up very loud. Troilus has a white towel the driver gave him for his hands, he hugs it to the stain on his chest. I have no idea where we are. Mother ought to be home at six. She will have a drink before she looks in our rooms. We stop at a set of traffic lights, I have not been smart enough to leave a note, mother will kill us.

The sign on the gate says it is the hospital though it looks like a very large home and we drive past cars parked in the driveway. The front garden is green, many of the trees have white scaled trunks and weeping boughs. It looks English. As we pass the trees, the gardens open to a lawn the size of a bowling green, white posts with iron rings stand in a square: I expect to see people walking dogs or cats, but there is no one. Yes, we pass a lady in black and white polkadots sitting on the grass. She looks very old. She feeds a Dalmatian with pieces from a wicker basket. She looks at us, and gets up onto one knee only with the help of a crutch that looks like a narrow stool. I cannot see anything wrong with the dog.

We back into a vehicular entrance at the side of the house and stop, the rear of the van flush with the brick wall. The driver turns off the radio and looks at me. Here we are, you go in there, and there is a lead-glass door marked Reception. Before I open the cabin door, he marks the clip-board and hands it across Troilus to me. The sheet is as narrow as a laundry ticket from room-service in the Apartments. Sign for the towels.

A battleship-grey limousine stands under the white-painted sign, Clients' Cars Only, a chauffeur's cap on the scuttle behind the windscreen. I look in. Glass divides the front from the rear. There are no seats in the back at all, the floor is a long cushion upholstered in diamond patterns bulging between the studs. A basket-weave of black tape hangs slack from the rear ledge like an empty parachute harness, and it takes a second to realise it is the safety-belt for a dog.

Reception is a regency lounge-room. In a corner at the far end sits a lady at an oak dining-room table used as a desk. Come over here, dear. Hullo, this is my brother Troilus and I am Cassandra. I will take your particulars. My particulars are my father's name and address, but he's away hunting, and his occupation, architect. What authority do you have? Mother pays for things by Bankcard, she will come and pick us up, I would like to use the phone. But it is my parents' cat, I say.

She writes on a clip-board. A short white coat over her day frock. She is not like anyone I know. Though perhaps The Spinster Aunt my mother called her, who used to babysit for us, not a real aunt, a friend of father's mother, she worked in an accountant's office for forty years and never married. In the winter knitting children's cardigans for the Sisters of Charity, let me try it against you for size, do stand still. She had a baby once, my mother told me, but never say. What is the cat's name?

What is the cat's name, she asks me. The cat is a vacuum, the name is a hole in the sheet. It is my parents' cat, old Gyngell will tell you it is, my mother will come to pick us up. She will know, she will not know the cat's name, she will not use her Bankcard to fill the blank, old Gyngell has not seen the hole.

The cat's name, says Troilus, is Batcat.

The telephone in the Apartment gives me an engaged burr. I will not know what to tell her, and put it down quickly. Thank you for letting me try, I will ring again later. The spinster hands me the clip-board. Sign at the bottom for admission, she gives me the pen, and this is the schedule of charges, let me try it against you for size, eighty dollars per day intensive care, recuperation days fifty, surgery per hour at a hundred dollars plus anaesthetic and extras. She marks them off. It is upside-down for her but her pen ticks quickly, she makes no mistakes. Do stand still. She expects me to be business-like, not a child.

Yes father, we can say it, a fortune, but we didn't know how much, they didn't tell us, it's not my fault. I turn up the ends of my smile and look directly at the bridge of the spinster's nose, honesty will charm her. Yes, I understand that, thank you.

The spinster leaves the room, opening the door to the barking and yelping of dogs, and is back quickly. They are doing what they can for, she looks at her clip-board, Batcat, but it is very sick, the skull is fractured and there is some brain damage. She hands me the clipboard. Sign here for the anaesthetic and surgery.

She leaves us sitting on the striped sofa, and chokes off the call of the dogs with the door. Troilus still has the towel and I should take it away, it looks very childish. I don't think I can. Over the mantelpiece, the picture of a white dog listens to an old phonograph speaker. There are thirteen other pictures, of horses and dogs and cats, each with the caption Royal Pets Through The Ages. They all look very fit. Why isn't anyone else in here?

I didn't notice him when we came in: a man sitting close to the door, the chauffeur, still as a grey shadow in his uniform. He doesn't look at us, his eyelids are peaked, the twin gables of old attic windows, no movement behind them as if he stays well back.

Troilus leans against my arm. The magazines on the coffee table are business journals and *Vogue*. I have seen the *Vogues*, mother has them delivered. I should ring her again, but I will wait. Colour brochures: your pet its health and beauty, Pet Holiday Apartments by-the-sea, early morning swimming and rub-down, we immunize your pet against home-sickness, unusual dietary habits catered for and piped music, and Pet Park Cemetery the largest in the southern hemisphere, through life and after life you care, by association with Hampton Park Monumental Masons in immortal stone. There is a yelping of dogs.

One, two men come in through the door, both in white coats. I sit up straight, no that is wrong, and I stand. Troilus only looks up. Is she all right, he whispers to them through a handful of stained towel. Is my parents' cat all right, I ask?

The two look very alike. A little early to tell, the one says looking at his clip-board, about the feline patient Batcat. We hope it will not become, he looks at the other, Requiescat. They laugh backwards and forwards. We have reconstructed the skull as best we could. One and one quarter hours at surgery rates plus anaesthetic, he hands the clipboard to me, sign for surgery and anaesthetic. Their heads lean together in sympathy. The one says it needs time, and the other nods, it has cardiac insufficiency. I do not understand him. The one explains, the heart is not pumping properly. The heart is a tired muscle and needs help. I shake my hair so it bounces, click, smile, click, yes I understand that, a heart would. The other nods again, cardiac support, he says. And pulmonary embolism, and the lungs are not clear. Oh, a hand over my perceptibly open mouth, click. Cardiac and respiratory support until we can gauge the extent of brain damage. Heart and lung machines, what do you want to do?

Troilus holds his towel in his lap. Will that fix the cat? She is valuable, my father likes that cat, and he looks toward me, not crying but his eyes are melting ice and his voice high. The one and the other both smile. They are Mister Broderick, father's friend and real estate, never beaten to a deal, masks at his New Year party, house right on the water, cost the mint today my father says, private jetty and tie your boat up to the party, a movie later only for adults, both stroking my hair. Their screaming masks hung against my wall into the new year, take them away mother, I can't stand it.

Troilus hugs the towel to his chest with brown fingers cracked by old blood, his face the grey of watching himself fall.

I wish mother were here. I did not know I had said it aloud, but Troilus's mouth is ragged, what good is she, he says, she's drunk. It is a pale cry, lonely as songs in his empty room.

I turn toward him, how dare you talk like that, learn to be more responsible, do sit up. Children aren't supposed to be here at all.

I sign. One and one quarter hours surgery per hour at a hundred dollars, anaesthetic ninety-five, ambulance sixty, oxygen hissing into his saffron tent, cardiac and respiratory support pumping blood and air my father knew the vintner, at seventy litres a minute, how much is that in metres and walk away before he thinks of it, surgical hoses bulging into a row of beads, how do you realise its value, the mask reconstructed as best we could, you can shoot them later, it wasn't my fault.

Thank you Doctor. I hand back the clip-board. Headup, click, pout, click, squeezing his damp fingers with my lacquered nails. Do what you can. And my mother's smile parts without creasing my cheeks.

Thank you, we will wait.

The Routine

I am sitting next to an imbecile. That's not kind, we don't label them now. Discrimination, categorisation, all that. But imbecile is right, perhaps clinically. A damp halo around his mouth, and wearing a straw hat in the aircraft yet. I'm too nervous. Jerky. Can't stay next to this.

Stalking me from the aisle, a flight hostess frowns without breaking her smile. Be kind, it all says, won't you. She's the one who must have arranged a window for his sliding gaze, shuffled him across my empty seat by his trembling elbow. Tied him tightly down, and withdrawn, he nodding absently away to the stiffening indifference of other passengers. Mortis de Rigueur. A window-seat needs one keeper but my nerves won't stand the jangling of keys. Be kind, her frown says; neatly repositioning the responsibility. Knowing I couldn't move to another seat, couldn't be so ungraciously quick with the grateful dead all around.

But I need time to be pensive. To calm my reasons for flight. Isolate a pattern of clicking chromosomes so compelling that to escape a lover I scramble through the hatch of any waiting aircraft. Leaving her sitting close to the phone. Again. I need time to play back sounds of voices raised far above levels safe for comprehension, to riffle through photographs glossy with misperceptions. Our early smiles through showgarden blossoms I said were fading. Our hands gripping over the clatter of wharf planks fluttering with disturbed

gulls. Counting the catalogue of our uneven steps between
colonnades in remembered museums. Fear had already cast a
wrongness to our poses.

Learn to cope, she said against my chest, with the dislocations of
your emotional faults. But I need the time.

After thousands of kilometres spent high above the globe, escaping
each city for the next,

State Your Reason For Entering / Leaving
This Country: Lost Job / Wife / Friends
(Strike Out Whichever Is Inapplicable)

and chance meetings on these flights become events to be valued,
particularly for a journalist. And a re-discovery that randomness is not
unpatterned. Over the last hundred flights, once sitting next to one
of Sukarno's jangling mistresses, and on another, to Milton Friedman;
to ninety-seven others who were, they claimed, neither.

To one nodding fool, his grin beckoning crooked as a bent finger.
De la main gauche.

He is going to talk to me.

No. Reprieved, as four hostesses mime the safety routine in mid-
aisle. Smooth hair and nylon blouses, a department-store showing of
the summer special. Safety orange.

Place over the head and pull
securely down. Inflate to this
season's bust size, thus. Do
not reach middle age until
safely clear of the aircraft.

For your own comfort, keep seatbelts. No smoking in the toilet.

He has been in an aircraft before. Letting down his backrest as far as it
will, into a dentist's chair. But he is going to ask something, make a
contact. And in a voice that will be a gurgling memory of tight
tooth-clamps and sucking saliva traps.

She said, I say, No Smoking In The Toilet. Yes, a very large airport, Sydney. International together with domestic. A Boeing, I think. Lots of colours indeed, green and gold, national colours.

Domestic means home. No it's not home for me either. I mean. I'll put your hat.

I wish he'd leave me alone. Fifty-two point four million dollars, this nation spends on institutions, keeping them in stainless steel doors and surgical forceps. Dry-cleaning the white strait-jackets alone must cost a fortune. They should be coloured. Safety orange. Fifty-two million, to tie their little friends tightly down, and then all into orbit safely clear of the cities. Well, they've lost one.

This flight is going to be difficult enough. All escapes are difficult; prospects of finding a fresh direction lessen with each increase in the need. An escape from another lover, certainly, but one of wit, and an apparent honest kindness that gives her midnight criticisms an unbearably rich veracity. She is fiction editor with a modest publishing house. You should, she said lifting her mouth from the red marks on my chest, exploit your best talent. She didn't say what that was.

In a voice wistful with regret, exposed my strained one-liners as a defaming of artistic integrity. Leave fiction well alone. Lie down until the feeling passes. And screw her to the mattress instead.

Artistic integrity. A fiction writer is a reporter who doesn't spell the names right.

And now I'm sitting next to this fucking freak.

The best passengers to watch are the practised sojourners, with as many hours in the log as some pilots. Not because they know the tricks of easy flying, but because they can skilfully abridge the most interesting parts of their lives according to the trip. The metronome of distance.

This is the five-hundred nautical mile story of my life. The eleven-hundred is shorter.

But most of them are going somewhere.

The jet-propelled ejector seat must be the loneliness symbol of our

time. Whizz. But there's nothing up there, doll. I've been.
This guy here has no left hand at all.

The only time I can talk to her is when she is grinding her teeth. And then she can't hear.

A mere routine, my lady says, of jokes in poor taste. So she will not help me publish. In case I'm giving her the runaround, another Routine? Maybe that's all I have.

He must have been in an accident. There is a wrist in there somewhere, and a round sac of wrapped fat that squeezes sideways strongly enough to be of use as a thumb. Crooked arm, a crab's forcep.

Snap and draw out the pale meat, tendons clear and stiff as celluloid. Wonder if he walks sideways? I wish he'd put it away. Who's supposed to look after him?

I needed to drop out of all that quick-on-the-drawers scene at the very time she wants to fly. But there's nothing up there, doll.

She's been a nice protestant girl all her life. Without sufficient break, that's part of the problem. Diligent at work and obedient at home. Married to a lecturer in optometry who lost interest in her after the birth of their daughter, and he didn't feel the tension. So shortsighted he couldn't read the big F at the top of the chart. Simply never noticed he had given her up for golf. Which is where I found her, contemplating her navel, just twenty centimetres too high-minded.

He has a strangely taut face, of indeterminate age. Either thirty-five or very old, pallid cleft chin and lumpy nose. Describe it with artistic integrity:

Bent as a 1930 Labor politician's/
Shapeless as a football after a wet game/
Hit by a Bondi taxi, the trams were on strike/
He is the other guy.

There.

No. Worse than usual.

He couldn't have been in an accident. It's congenital or thalidomide.
His good hand won't work either, poised forever just above his fly,
stretching out to touch. Hooked to his belt in a stainless-steel band.

Yes, I'll polish your spectacles. They wouldn't get smudgy if you
didn't push them on with your. Hand.

I haven't done so badly by him. Admired his retractable ball-point
pen, and sugared his coffee. Not that it's been noticed, the hostesses
don't seem to care, treating him as if he were anyone. The pen is
enormous, a foot long, a joke made for the useless-gift market. It
keeps toppling out of his pocket onto the seat between us, where he
pretends not to notice until I hand it to him. If I don't notice, he
nudges and looks away.

He drinks his coffee by holding it fast to the tray-table in the crook
of his crab's arm, bending down to it, and pursing his lips to make a
straw. Ssss. Two cups. And I'm right in line to have to take him to
the toilet. To undo the jacket-buttons, round red saucers, and pull
down the oversize plastic zipper.

Someone should have stayed with him. Who put him on this
aircraft. Don't ask me to take him. Just don't ask.

She is singleminded about it. More than a new toy. It has become the
new aesthetic, sexuality as the meltingplace of form and substance. I
would want to talk, and be smothered with a laughing pillow. Hey,
I'm more than just a pretty phallus.

In my case alone, I said, was the pen not mightier than the sword.
Another joke in poor taste, evidently.

Imbecile is a bit hard. Certainly not very bright, his gurgling voice
and the dew at the ends of his clown's mouth don't help first
impressions. But looking into him is different. I had expected a . . .
vacancy of gaze. A hollowness.

But his gay blue eyes. Light as a child's.

He's been to Bali, for christsake. Is on his way home. Yes a bit hot
for your own comfort. For Your Own Comfort, he says, flapping a
huge and empty sleeve about across his face. I mustn't laugh. But a

lovely place, Bali. And a toilet off your own room, yellow buses and shopping. That's where he bought the pen. It does go in and out, indeed. Clever.

And lovely, the people.

Who looks after him? To Bali on his own. A Bit Hot, certainly, particularly if your good arm is paralysed too, so that it lies there hooked to your belt, looking fine. So that something looks good, even if it is a fake. Of sorts. And if you wear your floppy jacket everywhere, like it or not, because you can't take it off.

Live with your family? No, live on me own. Used to be mother and he. But she fell over. Down the stairs, down the stairs he thinks it was. Bump, bump. And broke all her hips, the doctor says so. She stays in the hospital now, he can't see her. Nice though, and the people lovely. Happy, she says so.

A mother. How old must she be. Small and Irish, to stain him with such pale freckles. And she in hospital.

Or is she not really there at all, gone years ago, escaped the wet glare of those shining walls by fading away. A wisp of clinical vapour. That's the smell in hospital corridors: silent currents of escaping souls.

And they never told him. They didn't notice until she was gone for a month. Fading away, too light to crease the sheets. Mealtrays whisked out untouched. She transparent, a faded watercolour against the white bed, and undulating to the draught.

Like watching the sunset, never see the exact instant of disappearance. Just: gone. Mother's had the vapours.

He's having a shave! Shiny-backed, cordless razor rammed into the stiff blueing craw of his good hand. With the other, jerking up and down the thin stick forearm. I know some girls who would think that is something.

And he thinks it is something. Grin and nod and twinkle away. It is clever, and it's fun to be clever sometimes, we each know it. Yes very clean, a little around the back, here. Great.

Since when has this country been sending defectives to Bali for a holiday? Or anywhere. Not this community, not us. Grin and bear it, mate. Private Enterprise Hails Restraint In Public Spending. He's not even a consumer. Goes to Bali and buys a dollar-fifty's worth of funny

47

pencil, and a new razor. No clothes, he's too careful of them, special zippers, big buttons and all.

But that floppy jacket; he's been a bigger man.

Social security pension? Ninety-four dollars a fortnight and all the air you can breathe. He couldn't save out of that. Rent, food, heaps of spare underpants. Bump happily about the rounded edges of your room at home instead. Stay where you can find the toilet in the dark. Weet-Bix and jam down your chin for dinner. Plastic chintz melting to the window pane. Fools prefer the familiar.

The last time I was in Bali, was in Tokyo. The fifteenth floor of the Tokyo-Hilton. Lying silent on a dark bed with a young European prostitute married, she said, to a Sarawak freedom fighter. She working to support the cause, and his acts of immense bravery. And I trembling under the cool deftness of her long fingers as she loosened the practised folds of my sarong. Surprised, she asked where I had learned to wear it. I found I could not truthfully answer. In the face of her morality, proud as any puritan's, I could not admit the indulgence that must tarnish the reply, however brightly I gave it. Oh, around, I said.

Calmer later, and tired, covered by a cotton sheet against a cool breeze. Through the rattan walls, dawn smells from wooden fishing boats and knotted rope nets, and dew clear in the throats of climbing orchids. The grumbling of waking children. Children waking to the hoarse hawking of traders in early marketplace filling with baskets and shouted conversations and rice from fetid green terraces hung like trays from the sides of greasy mountain roads. In the lanes, slim groups of girls, brown and dry in the midday sun. You wan' see my bateek?

And in the temples, theatre. Theatre, ringing with brass gongs and patterned under the beating of musical hammers. Prancing slow behind fearfully carved masks, fingers rolled into scrolls in the air. Acting out the life and death of animal ancestors that were also ours. Holding high the meaning of our gestures.

Only for the villagers, squatting quiet as mute beggars in the aisles, indifferent to the stiffening Europeans on their hard benches, is this ritual a practised folding of time.

Expensive for you to go to Bali, was it? I imagined it would be. Lots of money. Yes, laugh, perhaps beautiful places do cost more. In a sense.

Take you long to save? Put money away for the trip. You have no money, no. I thought perhaps. But getting so far, takes money. How did you?

People. People help. Some people.

Some people, indeed. My kiss for yours, whoever you are. A person here, a person there. Stunned by the surprise of his gay eyes, too.

I don't think there is any more coffee. Sorry I thought you meant. Two cups, yes I did notice how many. The toilet. I understand, sorry, the toilet.

No, not an outside toilet. Yes, a joke. I wasn't thinking. Of you making a joke.

Not a bad joke either. More whimsey than my strained one-liners.

For your comfort, the toilet
is situated well clear of the
aircraft. Keep to the centre
of the slipstream, which is
frosty and overgrown by cumulus.

Sure I'll take you. Big zipper and red shiny buttons. Hold on to your pen. Lean on my arm and we'll shuffle out, the duplicated gaiety of a couple of comedians. I'll shake the hat and you hold the stick. The sideways soft shoe. Treat it all like a music hall. It's my role, too.

Pedigrees

I found Elinore Carver where I should have looked earlier in the night, in the poolside bungalow my wife Catherine and I call our Bower, sitting there in a cane chair at three o'clock in the morning. She was still drunk. The Bower was dark, but I could make out the open door of the cocktail cabinet against the wall. Elinore stopped shouting to herself only after I had stood in the doorway long enough not to startle her, and I saw the long cigarette butts that littered the floor at her feet like discarded marks of exclamation she had stamped angrily into the ground, having drawn from each of them the emphasis she needed.

She was nursing a bottle of my gin and the snug form of her dog, Prince Maximilian of Heathcote, whom we were always forbidden to call Max, and the repeating thunder of two days rolled over us, for it was to be the driest autumn on record and the skies could do nothing else. Under the chair, with her muzzle trembling against Elinore's foot, was the Countess Mystique, whom Catherine and I are permitted to call Misty because she is ours, although Elinore had bred her. On every thundery night, and on every November Fifth to avoid the worst percussions of children's firecrackers, Misty leaves her mat on the porch and hides here in the Bower.

'Elinore,' I said. 'Everyone has been looking all over for you.'

She wore the heavy sable coat she likes to call her Old Thing, although its value was then still more than her husband earned in six months. I was sure she shrugged, but perhaps I have only the vision of Elinore shrugging in that sable in gardens and at parties and at cocktails, whenever she thought it was appropriate to hitch herself free from some implication unjustifiably close to her.

'Fuss,' she said. 'Everybody is fussing.'

At about two o'clock in the afternoon, Elinore, happy on champagne after winning the first of two dog shows for the day, and driving a white estate-wagon banded with the same cinnamon and gold for which her miniature Shetlands are admired, knocked a child and his red bicycle fifty-five metres along the Northern Highway, and, by the time the child had finally come to rest in a stone culvert lined only with the shredding brown cuticle of ten weeks' drought, Elinore had already successfully negotiated the next bend and not one of the four roadworkers patching fissures in the asphalt had yet time to drop his shovel.

'Have a drink,' Elinore told me. 'I'm celebrating.' She laughed. 'With your gin. Sorry.' She felt around under the chair. 'I have a glass here somewhere. No. No, don't turn on the light.'

Thunder again; but further distant, somewhere out over the bay, and Misty was plucky enough to lift her head as I picked up the telephone.

'What are you doing?' Elinore asked sharply.

'Calling Horace,' I said. 'Only Horace. He came over earlier. He is worried about you.'

'Horace worries about anything. Horace is a fool.'

Horace and Elinore were married in the smallest church on the central plains. It had been taken from its colonial site and rebuilt, brick by brick, on the sheep-station owned by Elinore's father. Her people are Anguses, and around the renovated church and splendid homestead, their fine sheep country stretched for sixteen kilometres in any direction.

When Elinore's mother died, her two children were about to leave school. Duncan was enrolled in law, on his way to becoming, as it would turn out, the first Judge under forty-five years of age on the bench of the Supreme Court. But old Gordon Angus kept his daughter at home. Elinore was slight, but strong enough to be an equestrian of whom her father was proud, and her dark hair switched as she rose for the fences. While not yet out of her teens, Elinore commanded a household work-force of eight, and gave dinner-parties for twenty couples and a Woolshed Ball annually for four hundred prancing feet. At shearing time, more than a dozen sweating shearers and their drunken rouseabouts, whose feeding and bedding and laundry she outspokenly supervised, took time off from their swearing whenever she was within earshot.

Soon after the four-day celebration with dancing, lambs on spit, and parties by the river with which her father marked the passing of her twenty-first birthday, Elinore was sent to Europe for what Gordon Angus still called the Tour. He arranged that she stay away for a year.

Elinore lasted, on that occasion, eight weeks. After Spain, Greece, and the right-hand side of Yugoslavia, she boarded a flight in Belgrade and got off it in Sydney. A chartered Piper then landed her on the airstrip at the back of the homestead, and in a long russet skirt woven for a Macedonian winter and in high goat-skin boots, she climbed the fence rails to sit by her father who was then appraising, through a rising haze of khaki dust, a mob of two-year-old wethers as they clattered into the pen.

Gordon Angus affected displeasure, but he could make no stern fist of it until the following day, and, in any event, it was seen that they were seldom apart for the two months until he sent her away again. This time she sent back postcards from eight countries in thirty days and settled in London.

Since the Angus homestead was one of those to which touring royalty and visiting statesmen were taken on comfortable trips to the outback, Elinore had letters of introduction to the High Commissioner's office in London. She took a job there as a receptionist and guide. 'Je fais de grands progrès en français,' she wrote home, 'but il mio italiano è not so great,' although she hoped later to enrol in the fine arts school in Florence. Meantime, she enjoyed escorting Australian tennis players to Covent Garden and singers to Wimbledon.

Although Elinore had never been a player of ball games, her letters also came to mention golf. Australian golfers were then in the UK preparing for the Open. Her father received cards postmarked Cardiff and St Andrews. Evidently Elinore was following the circuits. Gordon Angus was too busy to ponder this deeply, for, although it was barely June, an endemic number of his ewes were afflicted with spontaneous miscarriage and small white corpses shone like stone cairns in the paddocks. Then, first from the telegraph operator and confirmed six hours later by delivery in a spattered courier-van, Gordon Angus received Elinore's telegram. Because it gave the flight number and time of her arrival, he knew something was wrong. It was in her nature, otherwise, to surprise him.

He met Elinore at Sydney airport. Although she seemed shy, she looked to him as luminescent as a movie-star, and people in the crowd watched as he clutched her.

Elinore asked if they could stay overnight in the city. Only when they sat over coffee in the restaurant on the twenty-first floor of the hotel into which they had checked, and she pressed her fingers over the back of his rough hand, did she tell him, as he had expected, that she was pregnant. He looked out over the lights of the harbour. The father of the child was Horace Carver. He was twenty-five, a celebrated amateur golfer, had no money just at the present time, but was shortly to turn professional. Elinore wanted to have their baby. Apart from her father, Elinore did not love anyone in the whole of the world as she loved Horace Carver. But what if her father could not come to like the man she wanted with all her heart to marry? The possibility terrified her. Perhaps their personalities were too similar. Perhaps she should wait to find out. Elinore was still within the time for which an abortion was reasonably safe. Although the practice was then unlawful, her barrister brother Duncan had telegraphed to her the names of Sydney abortionists. Three such addresses were written into the notebook in her handbag. As she slid her handbag onto the table, the time was eleven o'clock and the restaurant was closing. Elinore and her father were the last patrons of the night, waiters were setting tables for breakfast, and lights at the end of the room were dark. While Gordon Angus clenched his eyes tightly, and pressed his daughter's fist to the salty runs which were then dampening his fierce moustache, Elinore asked if her father thought she should approach a surgery in the morning.

Within the half-hour, Gordon and Elinore Angus checked out of the hotel and began the long drive west for the homestead.

Horace picked up his telephone so quickly he must have been resting his hand closely beside it. How long might he have been poised like that? A man playing snap with cards dealt to his wife. As much for Elinore as for Horace, I took care to speak distinctly. The times for secrecies seemed to have passed irrevocably long ago.

'Elinore is here,' I said. 'She was sitting in the Bower.'

'Tell him to stay home,' Elinore said. She poured herself a drink.

'She wants me to tell you that she is OK,' I said. 'But she seems to have been celebrating something or other, for some time.'

'Bitchy,' Elinore said.

As I put the telephone down, I was not sure if Horace had said anything at all.

'He'll come right over,' I said.

Horace's decision to turn professional was announced at the time he and Elinore were married, and it seemed that the quitting of his amateur status and his bachelordom together marked some new seriousness in the progression of his career. He was engaged by a small private course on the south coast, where he would teach businessmen at weekends and storekeepers in mid-week the serene back-swing for which he was notable. He then began his career with two sponsors: a sporting goods manufacturer who decorated his golf-shop with stock sufficient for a modest turnover, and Gordon Angus who decorated his bank-account with money sufficient to see him through the first year.

Gordon Angus also bought Elinore a house. The old man's lawyers constructed a trust to give Elinore rights of ownership *en severalte* – a term, as they pitilessly informed Horace, which excluded him. An hour's drive south of the city, and with two and a half acres of dandelions and green fescues around it, the house was separated from the Pacific only by the coast road and a narrow reserve of casuarina, ti-tree, and coastal gums which held the brow of the cliff-top together. From here, a sandy path, stencilled with the footfalls of sneakers and crescents from horse's hooves, ran down to the beach.

This is the sort of neighbourhood in which house-numbers are difficult to find. Gates and porches are hung with names etched into plinths of red cedar as if they are ranches. Property values accord, not to the sweetness of their pastures or to the vitality of their springtime rains, but to the views their papered lounges have over the Pacific, and, although the days here too begin for some at dawn, there are scarved women with daughters in pastel jeans exercising tubby ponies on the sand or running with dogs made beautiful and perfidious by their excellent pedigrees, and lonely men in gaudy shorts who, having run the beach until they are breathless, plunge beneath these waves which seem to have been made only a moment ago by the disturbance of the sun rising out of the ocean.

This, then, was the setting into which the child to be christened Judith was brought, eight days old and lying rowdily in a wicker basket strapped to the rear seat of Horace's car, while Elinore sat in the front hugging her knees as if she were cold.

Horace carried the basket into the nursery. The walls were hung with framed cartoons of good-humoured animals posing, as best they could, as their letters in the alphabet. On a bed which would not hold Judith for another eighteen months stood a tiny regiment of puppets and dolls and bears, and a black clown with a yellow smock which was to become Judith's imperturbable confidant. Elinore had arranged these joyfully, and with an eye to gay and rhythmic progressions of colour, and checked it all again before leaving for the hospital. Horace now expected her to lift Judith up and display to her the inaugural possessions of childhood, hoping for some artless gurgle which they would interpret as a sign of precocity. But Elinore put the basket into its frame, drew the curtains closed, and left. He found her in their bedroom. He suspected she might be tearful, but her eyes were dry. Elinore was gathering clothes from her wardrobe. She wanted to feel capable of sleeping with him again in this room, she said in so dispassionate a way it disturbed him, but meantime she would live in the guest-room at the end of the hall.

Elinore's physician was offhand about her depressions and talked briefly of a depletion of hormones. Horace gathered that he must simply wait it out.

The next six months of his waiting was confused by Elinore's sudden and inexplicable changes in direction. She restricted his visits to the nursery on the ground that it might interfere with the unambiguous development of the maternal bond – a concept she had read in the Journal of Nursing Mothers – but engaged Mrs Hagerty, a mothercraft nurse recommended by the hospital, to bathe and bottle-feed the baby. Elinore complained that Horace's teaching schedule kept him late for dinner. He arranged his morning class to hit off at seven, although it meant he left the house before dawn, and closed the afternoon class earlier. He was then always home before six. It worried him that Elinore did not notice the difference. He wondered if she might simply be lonely, but she would accept for them only two invitations to dinner in those months (in both cases Elinore was, as a host put it, Maman d'Honneur) and she refused other invitations weekly.

Horace and Elinore tried to talk their problem through. Perhaps they chose a time too late at night. Elinore cast about for something to say, and Horace was terrified that he might appear unable to keep his attention from wandering. He fixed his gaze on a furrow in her brow. Each time she began, she faltered away as if her sadness were nameless and imponderable, and talking merely destroyed the words she had hoped to use.

She managed to convey to him this: she had expected, in return for the efforts of motherhood, to find the small fragrances and delicacies of life multiplied and that the pains of self-sacrifice might cause her bosom to heave with pleasure; instead, her sense was only of dishevelment and loss. The terrain into which she had now wandered was a wasteland. Her own baby seemed, to her, soulless. Its cry reminded her most of the dry barking of a crow.

Horace sat straight in his chair. He did not seem to understand much of this. It would have been inconsistent with Elinore's new view of their lives if he had. Yet, he had a suggestion to make.

'Elly, I don't know a lot about women's troubles. But I think you miss your father.' He paused as though he might already have made his opening wrongly. Horace had a long and tanned forehead which, not uncommonly among Australian sportsmen, was tiered with creases as if it were once bound with thongs. At times of seriousness it seemed charged with the effort of thought.

'Go back home for a holiday,' he said. 'If you want to take Judith, you can. Or Mrs Hagerty can look after her here, and I can fill in on the days she is away. A couple of weeks, and you'll be right as rain.'

Horace took a breath and waited for Elinore to answer. He saw that her lips were momentarily unsteady, and her eyes held eddies which he thought flowed from gratitude.

'So,' she said, 'you are passing your responsibilities back to my father.'

Elinore's spirits began to rise as her car climbed to the rim of the plateau on which the Angus property lay. She was alone, and her appreciation of those moments did not need to remain adult. She had grown into womanhood here and the indelible fantasies and comforts of her childhood were all about. Sunshine fell through the trees overhead and she held her hand out from the window so that bright gusts of it blew over her palm. A flock of white cockatoos rose into the air in waves as though the noise of her approach had unexpectedly lifted them there and they screeched with ill-temper. Sheep in their roadside paddocks were smug and prosperous. Tree-trunks up which she fancied she had once climbed from the back of her pony were streaked, still, with the musk pinks and pale lavenders which had made them beautiful for her then. Dark herons she remembered as able to conjure frogs from puddles in which there were none unfolded sleeves wide with grey and white brocade and ascended, she saw, with faultless wizardry. It seemed to Elinore that these were the herons which had lived by these pools when she was a child.

Gordon Angus met her at the last gate. She knew then that he must have been watching, from the verandah, for the funnel of dust she left through the hills. He rode a tall bay mare she had not seen before and opened the gate for her without dismounting. This small display of skill made her smile and wish that she could swing up onto the mare's rump and hold her father about the waist for the canter home.

At the homestead, Elinore saw that the short ride had made Gordon Angus breathless. His hand, as they climbed the few steps to the verandah, was moist. She asked him about his health. 'Not bad for an old feller, Elly,' he said.

They sat late at the dinnertable. Her father seemed subdued. They drank, she noted, two bottles of claret and a half of brandy. She was not surprised that he became maudlin. His cigar droppings lay over the cloth. His cheeks were limp. He liked to remember the days of Elinore's infancy, and his anecdotes were long and repetitious. They were memories of gaiety and of childish irreverence, but Elinore could not feel, somehow, that her father was lauding her. The answer was some time in coming. Gordon Angus was hurt that Judith was not with them.

Elinore could picture Horace's evenings at home, on the nursery floor, his cheeks and his forehead wreathed equally in smiles, building pyramids of rag-dolls vulnerable to Judith's fist, retrieving rattles thrown far for the noisy fun in them, bouncing a coloured ball while Judith's gaze bumped along, one oscillation behind. When Elinore rang him, Horace was not happy to change the arrangements, but he was moved by the new liveliness in Elinore's voice. She was not slow catching on to it. 'Much better already,' she told him, 'but missing Judith, dreadfully, and this is all that could possibly hold me back.' And Horace agreed to drive Judith and Mrs Hagerty to the property, Monday he thought he could arrange, on the clear understanding that this was for a few weeks only, a month at the most.

Two months later, Judith was christened in the old colonial church at the homestead by a minister flown in with the guests from the city, and she was still there to celebrate, with much the same excitement, her first birthday. Although her first word was happily interpreted as 'Mama' like most initial and fortuitous syllables of children, her second was 'Bapa' and was reserved by Gordon Angus for himself. Horace had to wait for 'Dada' and this was unfortunately long in coming.

Gordon Angus spent more and more of his time with Judith. She held his finger during her stumbling walks in the garden. If the old man sat in the sunshine to read, he liked Judith to be playing nearby. Often he sat her in the saddle of a pony and held her in place while he led them around the house as he had done twenty years before for her mother. After an afternoon's work, he expected Judith to be the first to greet him. Very often she was.

Elinore was to think deeply about her own reactions to this only

much later, with the encouragement of her analyst and of Lysergic
Acid Diethylamide, and would then recall that during these months
she came to prefer wearing shorts or jeans rather than frocks or slacks,
chose to leave her hair girlishly down rather than pinned stylishly up,
and, when her father came into the house after a day's absence calling
for his 'little girl', Elinore was quick to assume he was asking for her.

There comes, now, part of an afternoon near the end of the summer
and, for the purposes of those stories which are still told in the dusky
parlours of some country hotels and in homestead kitchens, it begins
soon after the afternoon tea-break. We are talking of the long
summer, weeks before the true autumn came in, which, as most
remember, was in no hurry.

The air is hot and heavy, and overcast with the low cloud of dry-
weather storms. The hills closely north of the Angus homestead are,
where they are bare of trees, the colour of old straw. The slowly
splintering sounds of lightning cause the eldest of the Toohey
brothers, both of whom are working on the horse-yards, to look often
toward the ridge in case of fire from a strike, since that is from where,
he remembers, the fires came in the humbling summer of '67.

The Tooheys see Horace Carver walking from the house toward
the haybarn. He detours to walk in and out of the stone chapel. He is
dressed in white slacks and shirt, and resembles someone who is
running late for an appointment but is unsure where he is supposed
to go. As he reaches the barn, Old Gordon comes out of it. They each
turn, then, to walk in other directions, like two men no longer on
speaking terms. Old Gordon turns toward the brothers. He has
forgotten his hat, which, they say, he wears rain or shine. Even from
here his face looks flushed. He waves his arm. 'Toohey,' he calls,
'Toohey.' And since his courtesy is always to use the names men are
christened with, they then know something is wrong. They drop their
tools to the earth.

For Elinore, the events began a few paces earlier than the Toohey's
account. She has a clear picture of where everyone then was.

Horace sits on the verandah turning the pages of a magazine. He
drove up from the coast yesterday morning and is to drive home again
late this afternoon. He is already irritable about it. Because this is a

Saturday and they are off-duty, Mabel Hagerty and the cook Veronica
have taken the utility to drive forty kilometres to a fete at the district
school, taking with them jars of orange-chip marmalade and apricot
jam which Veronica will enter in the competition. Gordon Angus
lowers himself into a deck-chair on the verandah and breathes heavily
out. He is weary. His hat is pushed underneath his seat. Horace, who
is sitting in the old man's reclining chair, does not look up from his
magazine. Elinore is pouring them tea. Gordon Angus is a half-hour
late in taking his afternoon break. He will not wear a watch working
outside, and the sky is too overcast to see the sun. Horace, Elinore
thinks of it then, has difficulty distinguishing daytime from dark
without his watch.

And, with their next words, the events material to the real
apparatus of that afternoon begin.

'Promised to play hidey with my little girl,' Gordon Angus says.
'Where's she gone to?'

'She was out here,' Elinore says. 'Horace. Where is Judith?'

The hours, or the minutes, which follow hold instants that will
seem to Elinore to have occurred in no memorable order.

She is aware that the Toohey brothers are riding off, on White Sox
and Laddy, to comb the patches of wattle scrub closest to the house;
she has run already from room to room looking under beds and into
closets, runs through them again in case she has somehow missed a
bed or a closet; her father has let the dogs out, but they merely bandy
about in the yard waiting to be told which sheep to muster; the
shearing sheds, the stables, the machinery sheds, the chapel, are silent
and reproachful; her father kennels the dogs again, for their yapping
might efface the thin register of a child's crying; Horace's slacks are
smudged at the knees, and Elinore is shocked that he has wasted time
praying, but he has been crawling the spaces under the house; the
volunteer fire-brigade, which can muster thirty men, is fighting a
lightning-fire at Ramsey's (how does she know that, did somebody
telephone?) and will not be available before morning; yesterday's
bright garden is now drab, spaces between the shrubs carry
herringbones of searching footsteps, the flowerbeds are wastelands of
dispirited annuals; she hears a small cry, but the fabric of a
thunderclap folds about it and shrouds it from her; and when she

hears the cry again, holding her breath, the crow that made it follows it closely from its tree to the ground.

Of the chronology after that, Elinore is certain.

The light is beginning to fade and her shoes are wet. She stands on a thin apron of mud which surrounds the small reservoir they call the House Dam, although its waters are used only for horses and poultry. Its level is low. Reeds and fern which would normally beard its edges now hang along the embankment above her head. Wound about Elinore's fingers are the straps of Judith's sandals, patterned with daisies. These sandals Gordon Angus had found at the top of the bank. Mabel Hagerty and Veronica, in the long-sleeved frocks and wide bonnets they wore to the fete, wait on one side of the water, and on the other, the eight Campbell ducks, whose locality this is, stand stiff-necked and askew like bystanders at a neighbourhood tragedy. All four men are in the water. The elder Toohey is now beyond the centre and submerged to his waist. His brother is to the left, and, to the right, Horace, whose rolled trouser-cuffs are well under water, beside Gordon Angus, his flushed cheeks mottled also with grey as if he were suffering both sunburn and frostbite. Together they resemble a line of earnest and deliberate pilgrims fording some biblical river. Each grips a length of stick and steps forward gravely. Items they have already found litter the water's edge: pieces of grotesque and water-logged timber, three gasoline cans, the tightly inflated body of a brush possum, and a sodden horse-blanket with broken straps.

One of the Tooheys levers his staff to dislodge a mass that slips away through the dun swirl and back to the bottom, Elinore again rubs the smooth buckle of Judith's sandal as if it were a charm, someone else has come to the top of the embankment to watch what it is they have found, the staff raises it only terrifyingly slowly so that it breaks the surface uneasily and lies awash for a moment, rocking clumsily, and, before Elinore can grasp any sense of its shape, of its colour, of its (God!) creaturely form, it settles away, but, inexplicably, no one lunges for it again, they are all stiff, as though in the presence of a happening of such moment that they cannot move free of it, until her father breaks from the water and runs for the bank. Elinore turns. The figure at the top of the embankment, the person who, too, is standing still to see what it is they have found, is Judith.

Behind her are the poultry coops, no larger than dolls' houses. In one of them she had fallen asleep. Her lemon frock is crumpled and tucked up at the rear. Curlicues of chicken down hang from her sleeves and are in her hair. She rubs an eye with a fist. This gives Elinore the ludicrous and wonderful impression that Judith is not long hatched.

'Hiding,' the child says.

Gordon Angus is first to her. As Elinore, too, scrambles to the top of the bank she is aware that Veronica and Mabel Hagerty have started for the house so as not to impose their own relief over the family's. The Tooheys will follow. Horace is not yet clear of the water, stepping as high as a wading crane in an effort not to lose his plimsolls. Gordon Angus is on his knees. His arms are about Judith's shoulders. The child smiles, although she has understood that something terrible has been set in train. Her smile is cloudless, for she has made the cruel and stupendous assumption of the young that they are always blameless.

The strength of her grandfather's hug is beginning to make Judith uncomfortable. He appears to be stifling a deep cry. Elinore touches his shoulder. Why is it so damp? She untangles Judith from him. The old man sags to the position in which the deeply pious show gratitude before the Progenitor of Mercy. Instead, he is showing submission before whatever Being it is who had taken a malicious grip on the glossy chambers of his heart, and he is as powerless as if it were squeezing his soul.

The stories that were to live on in the hotels and the warm kitchens finish Gordon Angus there, perhaps in the interests of tidy storytelling. It was not quite so, but eighty-two hours later, alone in a pale green room in the District Hospital at four in the morning when that grip again took him, and when it let go he was dead.

There follows a period Elinore puts at close to twelve months. A dim and muffled interval like the rest between successive scenes of a play in-the-round where darkness indicates a passing of time but it is, surprisingly, not too dark for those re-arranging the set. When the lights came up again for Elinore, their house at the coast had been sold, Judith was nearly three years old and living with Mabel Hagerty in Duncan's town-house in the city, and Elinore's psychotherapist was, behind his sepia spectacles, suggesting that she take a holiday overseas.

So Horace took Elinore to Europe. Elinore is happy with that description of his initiative although the idea was not his. Neither was the money which satisfied their plane travel in first class, the snappy hotel suites, and the hire-cars. Horace had planned for six weeks away. To justify the tax-deductibility of some part of his costs he entered three modest tournaments in Spain, Belgium, and Norway. He spent his time sightseeing with Elinore rather than working on his form and only in Norway, where the Cup was won by an amateur who was also the Crown Prince, was Horace able to finish in the first half of the field. The next day they flew to London.

They stayed at a hotel which seemed to Horace to take up a quarter of the periphery of the square. It was pompous. The floor-staff wore livery made to designs of the eighteenth century although the hotel was built to glass and metal designs not yet five years old. The tidy young men at reception spoke to him in haughtily absent-minded tones when he asked for his mail. Walking from the lifts to the doorway, he hid his hands in his pockets and scrutinised the floor, and he appeared to Elinore to be more Australian and further displaced than at any other time. He could summon no taxis and was never sure how to tip for any item of service. London was not Horace's place.

But Elinore was welcome. Within three days of their arrival she had enough dinner invitations to fill ten of the fourteen evenings they planned to stay. Those with whom she had worked at Australia House sounded anxious to see her again. They greeted Elinore with gestures of warmth and immediacy which made her confident and talkative. Second and third level diplomats took them to lunch. There were days in the country. A surfeit of ruddy men in houndstooth jackets who were only briefly interested in golf, and quick-witted young women whose questions about Australian sopranos he could not answer, began to un-nerve Horace; but Elinore was again building a sure picture of herself with each new recognition in the way one strokes away mist from the face of an old mirror.

In the mornings they shopped. The day of their departure drew closer and the pattern of Elinore's shopping altered. She bought less for herself and began selecting gifts for her child. She had spoken of Judith infrequently. In all the time they had been away she had sent back two postcards, written with condescending clarity for Mabel Hagerty to read aloud, but she now searched out toys and nick-nacks from the shelves of shops and stores with ruthless and passionate lunges.

Her sudden obsession filled Horace with love and admiration. Doctors had told him that the most worrying aspect of her illness was the rejection of her child. It carried the implication that she blamed her child for her father's death. Now, this Christopher Robin, these Raggedy Anns, the Columbines, picture-books, hand-painted blouses, crayons the shape of the Seven Dwarfs, together seemed the most explicit index of Elinore's resumption of motherhood. After a few days of shopping, the fact that Elinore might find difficulty fitting it all into one suitcase was evidence, to Horace, that the newly healed bosom of the Carver family would soon be as cosy and rounded as any.

It was the day before they were due to leave. Their ten a.m. flight was to take them home via Lisbon, Calcutta, and Hong Kong. The brochures appropriate to those cities were already in Horace's coat pocket. His bags were packed. He had slid them out of sight under the bed so not to betray his anticipation.

The suitcase into which Elinore had piled Judith's toys would not, indeed, close easily. Horace sat on it like a potentate whose worth was to be matched by an equal weight in gifts and bounced to make himself heavier.

'When you give her all this, I'll take her photograph,' he said.

Elinore did not look up. Horace assumed she was already savouring that time.

'There's a thing you have to understand,' she said, 'How much better being in London has made me feel.'

'Sure,' he said. Horace was well used to the fact that he was without inexhaustible reserves of sensibility but he was surprised at so short an assessment as Elinore now made of him. He was not much pained by this. It emphasised the accuracy with which he understood her. He was proud that the distance between them was nowhere near so great as Elinore evidently thought.

'I would be blind to miss it,' he said.

'You give these to Judith,' said Elinore.

'Some,' he said. 'I'll give her some.'

'Everything,' Elinore said.

Obviously Elinore was underestimating the importance of her own rapprochement with their daughter. It troubled him. His forehead creased. Her over-generosity was errant and dangerous. But he loved her, so it was all capable of salvage.

'We'll give them together,' he said.

'You are not listening to me,' Elinore said. 'I am staying in London.'

Snow and Christmas fell on London on the same day. For Elinore both were grey and loveless. She had lived in an apartment in Kensington for a year and was, as she now puts it, between friends. Even at her most confiding she will be no more specific than this. Since Christmas is not a day for visiting acquaintances she spent the day alone. Cards from Horace, Mabel Hagerty, and her brother Duncan stood on the mantelpiece beside a photograph of Judith. Elinore had bought a card for Judith but it was still on her writing desk. She looked at her watch. The time was two in the afternoon. The sounds of laughter were blown against the window-pane as children ran in volleys through the windy street. She walked to her telephone. Since she had poured her first gin at midday, and was now on her fifth, she had difficulty in locating the international number. When she booked the call to Horace the operator advised of three hours delay and asked if Elinore realised that Eastern Australian Time would then be after midnight?

'What's it matter?' Elinore demanded. Her voice was loud and tearful. 'This is a mother calling her little girl on Christmas Day.'

Only after the return call had woken her from a shivering nap on the couch did Elinore remember that Horace had rented a beach-house on the north coast for the summer vacation. In any event, for Judith it was no longer Christmas Day.

'I'm sorry,' said the operator, 'I could book you a set time in the morning. How old is your little girl?'

'Forget it,' said Elinore. 'Cancel everything.'

From where she stood Elinore could see Judith's photograph. The message, in pencilled letters, teetered across the fascia like over-confident alphabet blocks. Since there was no punctuation the words could convey either a tribute or a demand. LOVE JUDITH, it said.

Elinore turned the picture to the wall and, by the time she left London for Sydney, Judith had already turned four.

The temperament of a neighbourhood changes. By turns it will grow vigorous, confident, ostentatious, blowsy, and then dispirited, as though there lives within it a signal and emblematic family with whose fortunes it must keep pace.

The Carvers came to invest (as people here like to call purchase) in our neighbourhood at a time when wrought-iron gates were replacing vertical slats, saunas in bleached Scandinavian pine and rock barbecues were filling awkward garden corners, and profits from the mineral boom had doubled the number of in-ground swimming pools. The equities and commodity markets were steady, three cars to a household was not considered flashy unless all were of the same European make, and the busiest shops nearby were patisseries and yachting chandlers. The Roads Department tolerated garden shrubbery which overhung the footpath and the most raucous traffic noises in the street came from bicycles and roller-skates. So few houses were owned by folk who were elderly that enquiry notices from anxious property salesmen littered their mailboxes like spurned bereavement cards.

In neither income nor prospects was Horace comparable with husbands in his neighbours' households. He had long given up teaching from a club, and, when others were busy in their offices with market analyses and management grids, Horace could be found on the ground floor of a city department store, behind the counter of its golf-shop, whose posters still proclaimed him the rising star of the national circuit. Eight years had passed since he had been well placed in any major tournament. But, since many men who are applauded for skill in business would just as soon be applauded for skill on the greens or at the net or beating to windward, Horace was granted that immune and classless standing afforded, around here, only to professional sportsmen.

Elinore was rapidly popular. She entertained generously and often, when a pedigreed bitch was ready to whelp she was never too busy to supervise and encourage it, and she lent her subscription copies of *Country Life* and *Queen* without hanging on their return. Although her behaviour toward her own husband was of condescension and reproof, Elinore gave other women no reason to suspect that she might covet their husbands. Her money had acquired for her a notable home and her neighbours were gratified that she also afforded a gardener whose skill reflected well the taste and beauty of the street. If she needed further acceptance, Elinore made sure of it when she organised resistance to a proposal that an orphans' residential school be sited nearby. She bought space for the campaign in local newspapers and debated the issue from the podium at a noisy public meeting in the Municipal Hall. When she was accused of heartlessness toward orphans, Elinore's mouth narrowed with anger. 'Not at all,' she said, 'I am an orphan myself.' She might have been asked at what age she was orphaned, but Elinore had given her statement with such belief in its legitimacy that the meeting ended without the question occurring to anyone. Her efforts were tireless and successful and all our property values were again safe.

When Catherine and I arrived at the Carvers' house-warming, the party was in full swing. Judith was not there and we assumed she was in some other part of the house, reading or watching television. Most of the guests were crowded into the billiard-room where there was a bar. The billiard-table had been covered in lace and stacked with food. In the darkness outside, the swimming pool was lit from under the water and glowed headily, as if it held the vapours which fill green fluorescent tubes. Waiters in dinner-jackets circulated around the room with trays of drinks and by eleven o'clock half a dozen couples danced on a square from which carpet had been removed to expose parquetry.

It seemed, then, that we were being invaded by boys who had heard the party from the street. Two shouldered through the folk on the dance-floor. Their ages might have been anywhere between eighteen and twenty-five. Their slick hair gleamed under the lights. One wore a denim waistcoat but no shirt. The other rhythmically clenched and unclenched his hands as if he were chewing gum with his fists. They made for the bar and began pouring themselves drinks. The dancing tailed away. There was a girl behind them.

'Don't mind us,' the girl said. Music from the stereo was a fox-trot. The girl made a face. 'We are definitely not staying.' Was there the suggestion in her voice that she could stay if she wished?

So this was Judith: thirteen years old and a reputation through four schools as a difficult child. She had lighter hair than her mother, combed so that it fell down one side of her face, and stained red at the tips, suggesting that it had once been brutally cropped and the contusions were still growing out. She held one shoulder low, in the style favoured by teenage queens of song and her mouth was indifferent to whether it made the signs of amusement or of disdain.

Elinore moved on Judith with the generous and invulnerable smile used by a hostess to greet a newcomer who was purposefully not invited.

'Darling,' she said, 'where have you been.'

'Nowhere,' said Judith. The boys snickered.

'Do up your blouse, dear,' Elinore said.

Judith laughed. 'Mother thinks I'm provocative,' she said to the boy leaning against the bar. 'Do you think I'm provocative?'

'Spunk-y,' he said and made a gesture as if he were rolling dice. 'Hey, hey, hey.'

Elinore turned away from him. 'Come with me,' she told Judith, 'I will introduce you to all our new friends.'

'Don't bother,' Judith said. 'We're going swimming.'

When Elinore saw, through the windows, the two boys throw off their clothes and dive naked into the water, she made for the switchboard behind the bar. Judith stepped on to the tiled rampart wrapped in a towel. The boys swam toward her. Their pale buttocks pulsed and wavered like jellyfish. They reached for Judith's towel; Elinore found the right switch; the lights went out.

Elinore turned again to her guests. Her smile was bright and clear. 'Those boys probably come from quite nice families, really,' she said.

It did not seem strange to anyone that, while Judith was sent off at the beginning of first term to a boarding school one hundred and fifty kilometres away, Elinore was taking extravagant precautions to prevent her dogs straying further from her than the front gate, but then, the corridors of girls' boarding schools flow with precocious children sent there for their own good, and I cannot think of anyone who believes that an affection for animals is not a fine index of the human capacity for love.

We saw little of Judith. At vacation times she preferred holidaying with the families of her friends rather than her own, and Elinore gave no sign that she was put out by it. Elinore's friends, on the other hand, spent so much of their lives enriching their children with ballet, music, drama, and dancing parties, that they banded together to share the burdens of transportation. At dinner parties, you could always tell who was on the roster because those women deserted the table at ten o'clock and sat down again an hour later, and no one asked them where they had been. We thought ourselves the sort of folk who might pause during an afternoon's walk in the garden to watch, with soft eyes and a requiting smile, the efforts of sparrows and starlings keeping pace with the deafening demands of their fledgelings, and the analogy of that sight with the impedimenta of our own lives signified a universal and continuing celebration of parenthood. It seemed, to us, sad that Elinore had not been able to find the same path.

These, then, are the directions in which Elinore's fortunes should have continued to run. In two years she had become one of five hosts on stately gardens open days and was proud that her rosewalks and shrubberies were so popular, she was active on the library auxiliary, and photographs of her dogs hung in the meeting-rooms of kennel clubs. Her life was otherwise unremarkable, save for whispers of a disturbingly headstrong daughter and Elinore's own capacity for gin and ice. Outside what home cannot comparable whispering be heard? These small worries had caused the skin over her cheekbones to shine, and the line of her mouth to loosen, a few years earlier than those of her peers, but she had slipped into a way of living which pleased her friends and which should have afforded her no unusual tragedy or notoriety, had her path not crossed, at two o'clock on a Saturday afternoon, with that of a child on a red bicycle.

Elinore and I sit in the Bower for the most part in silence, waiting for Horace to walk the one and a half blocks to us, his hand, perhaps, thrust deep into the pockets of his slacks, wondering if he should send a message of regret to the shamefully humbled family he imagines still lying awake in a cottage confronting the Northern Highway, if he should have notified the police that his wife – Carver, Elinore, Hit Run – is already found, slowing, as he turns the corner to pass the Rasmussens' until he sees that both storeys are in darkness although he had expected James and Margaret to stay awake in case Elinore called them, past the Peebles' gilded gate where a Labrador puppy belonging to one of their six children grizzles with loneliness, to Debbie Lake's, with whom Elinore has not spoken since Judith stayed there overnight on one of her tearful flights from home, turning then into my driveway, past the driver's side of my car and noticing that Elinore's is not there, skirting the pool, surprised, as he reaches the Bower, that it is in darkness, and realising as he enters the doorway that he has rehearsed no special words for Elinore.

'Elly. I've been looking everywhere,' he said.

'Let me know what you find,' Elinore said. The gin bottle gurgled thinly.

'It's been a wonderful day,' she said.

'Elly!'

'It is not every day that one dog wins at two shows.' She spoke into her glass, so that her voice sounded solitary and remote. 'A triumph of breeding,' she said.

'Elly, driving on to another show after the accident, it's not going to look so good.'

'I'm not going to discuss anything unpleasant tonight. Is Judith home? She promised to stay all weekend.'

'I sent her to Mabel Hagerty's. Until this . . . calms down.'

'Judith. There's another triumph of breeding,' she said.

'It is not Judith's fault. I sent her.'

'Nothing,' said Elinore, 'is ever Judith's fault.'

Judith is two and a half years old. She holds a doll firmly by an arm. The doll is a clown with a yellow smock. Because its face is black its name is Cindy. Cindy hangs askew like an acrobatic clown at a circus. It is a gaudy, self-sufficient and offhand performer, which may be why

Judith is seldom without it. Cindy's mouth is stitched permanently to express amusement. Judith's expresses neither this emotion nor any other. Her gaze seems too wide to focus on any one point. It is the gaze of a child who is unsure of the intentions of things she judges to be within striking distance, and unsure of the extent to which she is culpable for the happening of inexplicable events.

It is not long before sunset. Elinore takes the child's hand. They walk across the coast road to the sandy pathway which leads along the cliff and to the beach. This is the first time Elinore has left the house in the months since her father's funeral. They pass underneath a white signpost which bears, now, only the word Scenic, and, when they are gone, the beginning of an evening breeze rustles the trees.

An hour later, as nearly as anyone can place it, the headlights of a passing van shine briefly on that signpost, and on Judith who is standing under it and facing the road which she is forbidden to cross alone. The van stops and backs up, for the deliveryman has three children of his own.

The child is not able to find enough words to tell him what is the matter but draws him along the path toward the cliff. With the limp beam of his flashlight he finds Elinore. It does not seem to be fear of falling which has made her unable, by herself, to move, although she is clinging to the bole of a white gum which overhangs the cliff. She is intent only on a bundle lying on the rocks fifty feet below her. It is the sodden and dislocated body of Cindy.

It is to take psychiatrists three months of gentle prying to release from Elinore's mind the belief over which it has closed. This belief is that she has thrown her child over a cliff.

'Elly,' said Horace gently, 'it's time to go home.'

'God. Home,' Elinore said, but she got to her feet, holding her dog closely, although without affection, as if it were an inert and merely useful thing, like a warmer. Her shoulders were bent and in the dark she seemed less a bitterly drunk housewife than a woman who, by a passage of events rather than time, had grown into a disagreeable old age.

'I can never go anywhere without you following me about,' she said.

Horace took her by the elbow and guided her through the door. The air outside was dank and gloomy. A vast foliage of low cloud obscured the sky as densely as that of a forest, concealing, for the present, the bright and merciless eyes of the universe.

Inventory

F.E.D. – LITTLETON (AUSTRALIA) LTD

Inventory

IN EACH ROOM SHALL BE DISPLAYED THIS NOTICE
SETTING OUT IN THE SCHEDULE HEREON
ALL THOSE ITEMS BEING THE PROPERTY
OF THE COMPANY AT THE DATE CERTIFIED.

And underneath is his tangled-string signature, and a date not yet
six months old. This was his second decree after appointment to the
Company.

Showing a sensibility that surprised those who said they knew him
well, he has included his own room under the new rule,

Office:

HENRY E. C. LITTLETON, CHIEF EXECUTIVE

Your office must be, he remembers the words exactly, a strong
expression of your personality. He had nodded. Of course, he said,
and looked away.

Schedule of Contents:

1. PAINTING, OIL, TITLED
'GEORGE A. LITTLETON
M.Sc. F.R.A.E. F.R.S.'

The painting had been shipped from its London studio to Littleton's Sydney the day it was dry enough to travel. It appears to be a life-size portrait, and shows a pale man holding charts and a slide-rule. His mouth wordless, the charts speak for themselves. Its painter chose to represent him as about five feet ten, perhaps a little taller. Henry Edward Charles's father was barely five feet five at the time he posed for it. Hardly that tall now, despite the thickly built-up shoes he began to wear soon after his investiture. One London newspaper had captioned his photograph 'Midwinter sees shortest Knight of the Year'.

2-6. PLANTS, INDOOR:
DRAECENA (3),
MONSTERA DELICIOSA (2).

The growth rate of plants in Sydney would have delighted his father. The two Monsteras on Henry Edward Charles's inventory had groped higher in the few months he had watched them. Every three days, dust on their fleshy leaves was washed off with milk. Perhaps they needed the protein, it was said some plants were carnivores. He never touched them in case they inflamed his hands, allergies were quick to redden his skin since boyhood. A stuttering house-master at boarding school had warned of infections from masturbation, the word spent some time in his mouth, so Henry Edward Charles slept with his hands spread above the eiderdown, even in winter. He found the chill kept his fingers pale and taut. The habit annoyed his first wife. The second was grateful.

That wife had hoped to share with her father-in-law a love of gardening. She thought it might germinate affection between them, and spent days walking her livingroom reciting the characteristics of plants she knew he cultured. She tended her window-boxes. But, from the day of her wedding until she left London for Sydney, she was never invited to Sir George's home. Exclusion at Christmas hurt her particularly. Christmas was the time Sir George measured the growth of his own family.

The immediate Littleton family gathered for Christmas each year at its two-storey stone home in Kent. Old Sir George's later years had softened its corners with ivy. He received gifts from his children before Christmas dinner, this year standing before a spangled pine, a potted American Pinus Lambertiana the gardeners had carried into the hallway for the occasion from the South Terrace. The family loudly admired its vigour.

Horticulture was Sir George's recent passion. A hobby, he repeated to Henry Edward Charles, which synthesised the elements of commerce: genesis, production and display. Sir George brought to gardening a gentler touch than startled his Far Eastern Developments Limited into a forced growth after he grasped control of the Company in the great Depression.

Sir George did not give Christmas presents. He had, he said testily to his wife, given his family all they had. How they spent it was their affair.

Simon G. and Margaret Anne had never attempted to choose gifts for their father's severe taste. They leaned on Lady Anne's whispered suggestion. But Henry Edward Charles always chose a gift himself. Holding it in the sweating hands of his adolescence until the silence was too much for him, his lips glistening with apprehension. As the others moved toward the diningroom he thrust it into his father's averted hands and then stepped quickly to mother's stiffening side, brushing from the shoulders of his suit the white powder he had smudged from the tree. Sometimes his father was clearly unable to open the carefully wrapped present at all.

Christmas was also a time of accounting. A biblical accounting, Sir George said after grace from the head of the refractory dinner-table, for talents bestowed by The Father. Lady Anne watched Henry Edward Charles's face tremble.

Emily, in the red kitchenmaid's pinafore she wore only for Christmas, lowered the basted roast to Sir George's side so he could approve it. Wonderful, he said, and nodded. The lines around her eyes creased, and Sir George watched her bob with gratitude. For thirty years a treasure. Accounting for talents, he announced, and began to carve deeply into the steaming roast. Margaret Anne, he said.

Margaret Anne smiled. Her suited figure, M.A. (Oxon.) and Ph.D (Stirling), was well known to Southern Africans. Their tribespeople gathered in the villages to wait gaily for her arrival, though she thought she was unannounced. Her project was to research the uses of drama techniques from the new London primal theatre as a substitute for language. It made them laugh. Her thin face was serious, but giggling crowds followed her everywhere. The British Journal of Anthropology thought her innovative, and she quickly saw its wisdom. Margaret Anne finished recounting her academic year, and began again to eat.

Simon G. smiled. Father knew his legal practice was now solid enough for him to rely on his three partners, and proceed to preselection for the Commons. He was, he bowed his tidy head slightly in thanks, grateful for father's patronage and for that of his father's warm friend William Cassell, Conservative party whip. Simon had made his special interest the extra-territoriality of offshore waters, and he championed proposals to strain planktonic protein by billowing huge muslin sheets across the ocean's currents. He would form a backbenchers' committee. Only the simple polyp, he said, could be called a true colonist of the sea. He had a background in strata title.

The panelled walls clinked to the silver sounds of their cutlery.

Emily entered the dining-room and began to clear the table. The family was silent. She gathered the engraved condiment cellars to her tray and left the room, closing the door behind her. Henry Edward Charles folded his napkin.

But Sir George did not wait for Henry Edward Charles to recount, over the remains of the goose, the imminent failure of his second marriage, six years old in January; or the collapse of his racing stable, a draining of the finest blood ever exported from Ireland and New Zealand; or the sale of the few remaining blue-chip investments to pay his slandering creditors so he could remain in his club.

This year – they leaned forward to catch Sir George's softened voice – it is appropriate to bestow a new talent. Henry Edward Charles is to be placed within the Company. Appointed to a subsidiary consistently profitable, as the financial press applauded in reviews, because Sir George's mineral extraction techniques were so acutely ahead of their time. To be appointed Executive Director, F.E.D.-Littleton (Australia) Limited.

Lady Anne felt her son bow his head. You are, his mother haltingly breathed, to be given a continent.

7. WALLMAP, RELIEF:
'DISTRIBUTION OF MINERALS
IN AUSTRALIA'.

By the beginning of February, Henry Edward Charles and his family were in Sydney. His wife disliked the heat, and the four children of his two marriages whined over the loss of their skiing month in Chamonix. The eldest daughter wore a padded Tricolor jacket everywhere, until a dermatologist diagnosed heatrash, though her mother suspected tropical disease.

The Company leased a home for them with a view of the Opera House, and on the southern side of the harbour, but Mrs Littleton found the morning glare, as she put it, troublesome. Their lawn sloped all the way to the dampness of high-water mark, which made the salinity quite out of the question, she said, for the amber shrubs of her childhood, and the colonial interior of the mansion was impossible. She would search for a designer, not an Australian. Indeed she already knew of one whose practice was fashionable, she whimpered over breakfast on the terrace, both in Double Bay and in the commercial canyons of North Sydney. Mrs Littleton was at her most tearful in the mornings.

So Henry Edward Charles's office was also designed by the American architect whose degree cost him twenty-one months and thirteen days, and whose qualification was rejected for registration anywhere outside his homestate. He had snarled and sold his flair in Australia and New Zealand by decorating master-bedrooms that reflected, he said in a gravelly drawl his middle-aged clients thought sensual, the alter-ego of the mistress of the house. That mistress was always surprised at the amount of alter-ego he thought she had. Often hand in hand they later re-designed the office in which she thought her husband spent too much of his time. Mrs Littleton found she mentioned it twice, fearing he had not caught it the first time.

Redecoration of the office was entirely complete within three weeks. When he was advised of it, Sir George telexed from London. NO DBT COY IS RUNNG SMOOTH AS CLOCKWK, he said, & CHF EXEC OFF IS FST PRIORITY STOP CONGRATS END.

8. FIGURE,
FREE-STANDING.

To the right of the door stands the gift from his mother. The armour of a warrior responsible for the battlefield successes, his mother had whispered, wrongly attributed to an early Littleton. One of four, articulations wired, that stood in fealty to the family corridors for as long as he could remember. He has hated them from childhood. Each day he forces open the visor's slitted gaze to extinguish its phantom. The grate holds with a rasp, still stiff to his short fingers. Each morning he finds it closed again. He has never said he suspects the cleaners of mocking him.

9-39. WORKS,
ARTISTIC (31).

Impressionist watercolours spatter the walls. Henry Edward Charles had thought the collecting might be fun, but the dealer was stern with responsibility. I have assembled for this office, the dealer had said, the most comprehensive collection of twentieth-century work presently in the country. He unsmilingly recorded Henry Edward Charles's chaste promise to allow the National Gallery an exhibition.

Henry Edward Charles's first wife had clutched his hand during her silent bids at weekday Art auctions. He feared she nodded with an excited vigour that cost him more than it should. Set your ceiling first, he told her in a voice he remembered from his club, and stick to it. So their house filled with their second choices. She had sold them all before their divorce decree was made absolute.

40-55. DESK, TIMBER (1),
TABLES, COFFEE (3),
CHAIRS (12).

Monographed H.E.C.L. in gold, his desk is placed, as he understands the theory, so the curves of the wall draw the eye toward it. Placement of the furniture is neatly balanced. He sees that each time he enters. His secretaries always refer to his room as The Office. Now, so does he.

56-59. BOOKENDS, CHROMIUM (4).

His desk is the size of a double bed. At the head and foot, small chromed bookends hold half-hide volumes of *Transportation of Convicts to Early Australia*, and *Indigenes and Contact*, given him by his sister. His brother had promised him something later. The spines of the books are still crisp.

60. CALCULATOR, DIGITAL.

The desk's refractory top, he will tell you if you admire it, was hand-turned by craftsmen from a single piece of the largest Blackwood ever discovered still standing in Tasmania. He had a square cut out of it so an electronic calculator, programmed to twenty-two algebraic functions, could be mounted flush.

His secretaries have never seen Henry Edward Charles use the calculator. They are to see it today. He has called a crisis meeting of Littleton executives. Shipping Division delivered, by liveried courier direct to head office, their forecast effects of rising oil prices. They watched the courier as he delivered it. He was agitated.

The courier had worked as the Littletons' chauffeur since their arrival in Sydney. Sweeping them to the very front entrance at opera and ballet, carrying HECL to the golf club, on two occasions delivering Mrs Littleton's gentleman caller home before returning to the club for the master again. One autumn afternoon, driving the eldest daughter from her private school to dressage lessons in the country, she tapped the dividing screen inside the Daimler. Her small fists pressed white discs onto the glass as she directed him. He delivered her to the gay flowergardens of a secluded hospital known for the discreetness of its abortion practice. He had to lend her another fifty dollars and leave her for three hours. He spent them kneeling before a statue of the Blessed Virgin in a nearby church. The courier knew more about the Littletons than any one of them.

He left the report with the secretaries and disappeared. It contains an appendix thick with extrapolations of cost increases to other divisions of the company. There is a covering note typed in clear sentences stating the conclusion simply.

Sitting behind his desk, Henry Edward Charles waits for his meeting to assemble. He has nothing to do. He should have fixed the meeting for an earlier time. It will be too long before his door will open.

61. SHIP, MODEL.

In the centre of his desk the funnel of a two-hundredth scale replica of the M.V. Sir George Littleton Venturer produces lighted cigars at the flick of a switch when his secretaries, who call him Dr Heckle because of the monograph but only behind his back, can be bothered to fill it. He finds it is not filled now. On a floor below him, the courier's warning flows the corridors, quiet as a film of oil.

62. CLOCK, PENDULUM.

His staff will arrive precisely on time. They have seen his irritation with timelessness. Time, he remembers the words, is the inventory of opportunity.

Sir George's study had held three hundred and twenty seven clocks and watches. Their time was set to an earlier passion. The young Henry Edward Charles did not own a watch. His mother whispered that she could not buy him one. She had spent hours browsing hushed watchmakers' shops in London, but Sir George's endlessly accurate knowledge of pivots and gearing and incabloc inelasticity sucked her imagination dry. She became suddenly frightened at her repeated indecision and fled the glassed trays of Roman and Arabic faces into the crowded streets without closing the door behind her.

Henry Edward Charles stood before his father. Though he was not yet twelve, they were the same height. Sir George's taut face was grey. A gold fobwatch, revered in the days Boswell wrote his journals, was missing from the collection. Its place was silent. He had questioned the servants. They had been in his service for years, for longer than Henry was old. Henry Edward Charles could hear the watch ticking. He did not know, he said, anything about it. His mother whispered to Sir George that the boy was telling the truth. We are too close, I know he couldn't do this thing. She took Sir George's shaking arm and guided him into the lounge.

After his father had been enclosed in the black Daimler and left the circular drive for the factory, Henry Edward Charles stood in his mother's dressingroom. It smelled of the powder he knew when he nuzzled her shoulder. He plucked at his pocket. He had difficulty retrieving the watch from it. Tips of his fingers found the links of chain and drew it out in a glittering parabola. He lowered it into the embroidered make-up case Sir George had given his gay wife on their honeymoon.

The boy did not know how his mother disposed of the watch. She never spoke of it again.

Henry Edward Charles now displays everything he has. The clips of his fountain pens array along the sill of his top pocket. His wife tells him this is unfashionable. He carries his wallet and a plastic folder fat with credit-cards openly in his hands. Envelopes are made to protrude from his side pockets.

63-70. DESKTRAYS, WALNUT (8)

His walnut desktrays tumble with paperwork. The cavernous drawers of his desk are locked and empty.

He has made the penalty for larceny from the company unappealable dismissal. It was his first decree.

Henry Edward Charles had not seen them enter. Suddenly the room is quietly full, he does not know how long they have been there. His secretaries are silently passing around cake and coffee, then close the door behind them. The meeting makes no move. The panelled walls clink to the silver sounds of their cutlery.

This report, Henry Littleton's lips tremble to the meeting, shows that consolidated operating revenue will drop in the next twelve months to fifty percent of last year. He riffles the stiff pages but lets the volume drop. Fifty percent of sixty-two million four hundred and fifty thousand is, it takes them a second to see he will use the calculator to compute the sum, is thirty-one million and two hundred and twenty-five thousand. The accountants receive the figure and pencil it dutifully in.

Do you know what that means? He shouts, as close to uncontrollable as they have seen him. Henry Edward Charles looks about the walls. They are no more faithful than the room his mother had decorated for him as a boy.

They lean forward to catch his softened voice. It means, he is having difficulty retrieving the words. He plucks at his pocket and draws out a gold fountain pen, lays it across the pages of the report. It means, he says, there will be a time of accounting for talents.

They sit still. It is some time before they realise the meeting is over, that it was an act of leadership, mother, a test of their competence, their talent, how they use it is their affair. He watches them quietly begin to leave. The last closes the door behind him.

The door is of Lebanese cedar. Its perfumed grain is locked behind a polyurethane glaze though it never sees the Australian sun. Screwed to the back of the door is the Inventory, mounted in an aluminium frame. The border of the document is very white, the lettering crisp as the day it was typed. It was sprayed with a colour fixative and has already lasted longer than the rouged typist who made it.

I Keep Meeting my Grandfather

The Solicitor spoke again the last words of the Will, with the halting wonder through which only lawyers can unsmilingly ponder the very clearest of statements.

'And I hope this is not all that Elspeth inherits from me.'

He turned over four of the words separately in front of us. The Colonel, my father, sat erect.

The Solicitor rolled back into his squeaking chair. 'No,' he said. 'No,' drawing the word out so that it was slowly fuller in its meaning than words of many more syllables, his parchment face framed with those six of his exact predecessors hanging on the wall behind his desk; and his opinion was their collective judgement.

'Unusual and, one may have thought, odd. But invalid? No.'

The Solicitor's desk was laid with thirty-two files stamped with the words 'In The Estate Of', bound with musk-pink ribbon tightly into the buckled shape of those paperbark cylinders in which some tribespeople roll the bones of their ancestors after cremation. My grandfather's lay face down in front of him.

'And if it was, that clause alone could be struck out without affecting,' I thought he smiled to himself, 'or infecting the other clauses, Colonel.'

The Solicitor did not smile often. Perhaps another dozen unopened files lay on his bedroom table. He slept alone, and all Glendale knew his wife spoke to him only in public, since he was interrupted in

flagrante delicto by the speechless husband of a rumpled and
trembling client, for whom, he wept, he had become unaccountably
amorous during matrimonial counselling. In a gesture of penitence he
changed his practice from divorce to probate, but my God, Molly, he
waved a client's yellowed testament in his wife's face, even the dead
are not as unmercifully silent as you.

'Curious,' the Solicitor said, 'I never before knew his real name.
Glendale knew him as Doddie. GranDoddie seemed to be his full
name. I think I have him in my teledex as Mr G. Doddie.'

Of course GranDoddie was my childish name for him. He responded
to it with a rush of pride that made him awkward, as if it were not
caused merely by the unformed lips of childhood, but carried the
intense understatement of love and admiration that glows into a
diminutive. He held the name to him, and all the reddening anger of
my adolescence could not wrench it away.

I paid him little enough attention in nineteen years: the overlap of
two lifetimes. Little enough. And now he has left to me everything
he had.

During the years in which a teen-ager feels the eyes of the world
burning on her cheeks I hated to be seen with Doddie. Outside
Supermarkets he jumped the pavement squares and hop-scotched back
again. He walked the tops of brick fences, exploded from the
doorways of arcades. There's not enough fun in this life, he said. He
spoke to prim and burdened women in crowded delicatessens, people
don't speak to each other, he said. I looked away.

Doddie.

The Solicitor turned toward me a face scribbled with the fine
calligraphy of his clients' worries. 'Elspeth, many in Glendale will feel
your grandfather's passing with sadness, if some relief. Relief,' he
looked down quickly and mumbled it, 'that when he died he was in
the best of health.'

I was, I knew, the daughter GranDoddie had lost. Though mother
was his early child, the thin wife of his bedside photograph had died
with the effort of her birth. Mother grew up wearing the white gloves

of a Presbyterian boarding-school during the terms, and in vacations, the pinafore of a servant to the unquestioning household of her guardian aunt, a careerwoman in government service who expanded her department with an entrepreneurial deception of her masters; creative obedience, she called it.

She allowed grandfather to visit his daughter for one hour, twice a month, and spent the next days correcting, her mouth squirmed, his anarchical influence. She forbade him bouncing his daughter on the nape of his ankle to the Banbury Cross canter of a white horse – it's indelicate, she said – and interrupted their final minutes of play with such suspicious discovery that the child stood, white-frocked and trembling, for an hour before his expected arrival. It took more than five years of her aunt's death before mother was calm alone with her father. In the sixth year she married, and her fate, GranDoddie always said it quietly, was complete.

He died alone in a three-roomed weatherboard house, it must have been built before he was a schoolboy, on a bushily treed slope behind our house. It is secluded and has a view of the creek.

And I hope this is not all that Elspeth inherits from me.

'It is this property alone,' the Solicitor leaned forward, 'that is central to your interest in the validity of the Will?'

'Central,' the Colonel said, 'yes. Central.'

The Solicitor leaned again back to his ancestors. 'What were the exact words of his undertaking?'

'That the property would pass,' the Colonel's throat could only scratch it out, "back to me when he died." '

'Not quite those words,' I said, and the Colonel looked at me with quick surprise, 'but that the property would not pass out of the family.'

'Ah,' the Solicitor said, and then to the Colonel, 'Is that your memory also?'

'Possibly,' the Colonel said more quietly, 'possibly'.

The Colonel thought of himself as an investor. I float my fortunes on the rise and fall of the market, he said, as if it were a tide. As if you were scum, GranDoddie said.

The Colonel had spent his Sundays motoring the gravelled roads of newly sewered estates searching for the opportunity of his lifetime. Unexpectedly, he found it in Glendale.

An old apple orchard, owned by a woman recently widowed, he chortled, so she can no longer work it profitably and has to take the tree-bounty – excitement bubbled like cider in his throat – for each tree winched out, now she can't stand the sterile mounds of earth in rows like a cemetery and wants to move to the city. A gift.

Mother was calm but the tension unsettled the Colonel. He did his sums over dinner, poking the forgotten scraps of beef into his mouth between pages, though he was usually finicky about hot food. Mother hovered at his elbow like the military batman of his officers' mess. He threw down the fork. The totals were impossible.

He added again overnight. He allowed mother to help. It was not inachievable, but risky. Interest and repayments would be very high. Unless, they thought of it together, GranDoddie.

GranDoddie threw them out. I will not use, he shouted after them, my war-service entitlement to filch land from a widow. He threatened to write to her but the Colonel had not yet said where she was. GranDoddie wrote instead to the newspaper. His letter was not printed.

They mortgaged themselves dry. Through the Solicitor, they commissioned a package-designed brick house and personally supervised the departures from standard, wandering the growing parapets each morning and night, poking the grouting for defects. On rainy days they stood ankle-deep in despair, the Colonel prising his platoon of contract bricklayers from their hut in his voice of a parade-ground – volume with dignity he called it – and complained of their slackness. To save costs they moved in early, though the builders had not finished, and I visited them from the refuge of my boarding-school.

It was not until the cost of variations and of time lost by their early occupation were accounted that they realised their first sums were right. It was impossible.

Two days later the Colonel tore from his mail a council notice demanding the first of three installments for the proclaimed sealing of the roadway. I don't want a macadam road, he shouted.

GranDoddie was suddenly magnanimous. Now I am dealing with professionals, he smiled. I will be able to move from my apartment, and he bought the rear half of the allotment from them, including the old homestead, at the first price the Colonel suggested, not using the war-service loan at all and signing the transfer slip from a savings account with such an obsolescent serial-number the Colonel was surprised. He's had it for years. I like to pay cash, GranDoddie said.

Another thing, the Colonel told him, I'd like it back when you die.

The rear allotment was overgrown and remote, and its value was less than a third of their outlay, but it paid off the most expensive of the mortgages. Their finances were again comfortable. Their purchase was restored to the status of a killing.

GranDoddie mounted the old verandah and stowed into the weatherboard house his every possession. The oiled floorboards bowed. He had never sold anything in his life, he said, ignoring the impossibility of it, I never had anything I didn't love.

Eighty years of climbing roses had knitted above the brim of the verandah and its pitched roof settled over him, kindly as a sun-bonnet.

For most of the week he kept to himself and resented mother's early attempts to supervise him. I am old, he told her, but healthier than you and that Colonel will ever be. He often referred to my father as That Colonel, as if he needed to distinguish him from the legion of a rank that wars were waged specifically to produce.

Saturdays GranDoddie entertained his own guests. The friends of his fifty-eight years as printer and publisher, the ragged typesetters whose stained fingers were blue with the cold of their dead trade, the writers remaindered after the sale of the Old Left. Their midnight songs rattled the windowpanes.

On Sundays he visited us. And I don't have the heart, said the Colonel, to discourage him.

The Solicitor read it out: ' "After payment of all my just debts (of which there are none) and my testamentary expenses (which ought to be little) . . .". An argumentative turn of phrase,' he would have thought, 'quarrelsome, almost. I must have met him on five or six occasions, though each might have been for the first time. He was,' he paused, 'agile.'

Yes. Agile.

The Colonel had become active in public affairs. He was an executive member of the Returned Servicemen's League and wore the gold badge of office in his buttonhole like a Flower of Remembrance. I have seen active service, he often said, from the rainforests of Asia to the deserts of northern Africa in the last world war – my second war GranDoddie smiled – and am proud, the Colonel said, to have twice stood for Liberal Party preselection – and twice failed, GranDoddie smiled louder.

To Sunday lunch the Colonel invited the contacts he plucked from his week. Do you collect, GranDoddie asked him, only people of recognised pretension – the Colonel turned away and GranDoddie called after him – because their weight is greater than the less dense majority?

I was allowed to escape the listless quadrangles and bored libraries of boarding-school for one weekend a month, and told Sunday-night dormitory stories of those lunches. Of the aged but burly-hipped widow to a ballroom-dancing fortune the Colonel hoped would partner him in a fund-raising drive, but it takes two to tango, GranDoddie laughed and only I laughed with him. And a criminal court Judge who was also the Grand Master of a Protestant secret society, though every Catholic lag, GranDoddie told him, knew it. And most vividly, the millionaire owner of the SeaQuarium, whose spine-teethed eels and mindless sharks bloodied their tanks at feedingtime twice daily to the delight of thousands – GranDoddie quoted the cost at him exactly: eight dollars fifty a head – and who spent vast sums on newspaper advertisements advocating the abolition of taxes and the survival of the fittest.

GranDoddie's was the grin of a dog after scattering sheep.

He forced discussion toward argument with the menace of a slowly drawn sword. Discussions begun over soup became arguments over coffee. Discussions begun on the lounge became arguments in the study. He became better at it as he aged. I watched discussion become argument before his sentence had fully left him.

As the topic turned to the war of capitalist expansion in Asia he sighted the emotion of pacifism against it like a gun. He bled the vivisectors weak. He undercut the champions of mining at Gove and Aurukun until their shifting arguments slumped in on them like sand.

And the Colonel's lips would pale.

Doddie!

He embarrassed us all. But I kept his silent score, following the points wherever he slammed them, with the vacillating eyes of a tennis buff. There was seldom a re-match. His opponents stumbled away from the Colonel's apologetic handshake trembling and angry.

The last of those lunches was less than eight months ago. The Colonel had held them, on and off, for five years, with longer pauses after the most disgraceful.

The weather was very warm. Mother had set up the lunchtable in the garden. Al fresco, she said, was now fashionable on the larger properties of Glendale. It was her first mistake. Their guests arrived in gay long dresses and cream-coloured suits. The women's pale shoulders reddened, the men dampened with steam. GranDoddie was comfortable in shorts and an open shirt, his knobbled legs brown, his white hair yellowed in the sun. The weather had presented him with an early advantage and the unfairness of it glinted happily in his eyes.

The drawcards for GranDoddie's evangelism were three.

The real-estate developer was a neighbour. For six months he had complained he could not enforce the clearing of native bush inside GranDoddie's boundary, despite the repeated issue of council orders proclaiming it a fire-hazard. It appeared on the council work schedules but was never reached. The foreman pointed to his heavy workload and shrugged. We'll get around to it. At the time we were all lunching in the heat, three council-workers, their wives and bare-bottomed children were picnicking under the cool lacework of Melaleuca and Cootamundra they were bound in duty to bulldoze into crackling windrows.

The developer left early, and until then conversation was light. GranDoddie prodded it along, but they were slow in the heat, ate little, and kept their lips pursed like beached molluscs, GranDoddie said later, to prevent the unnecessary escape of moisture. The Colonel adjusted the red and green sunshade for the ladies.

Mother thought we should expect a hot Christmas. She saw her second mistake as GranDoddie nudged us through Christmas toward religion.

Christ was the only unrewarded Christian, what do you think of it Pastor? After the crucifixion his ministry knew a good deal when they saw one, and turned it into a franchise.

The Pastor's smile was a mirage in the heat. His new Church of Christ the Benefactor was the highest rated religious television programme in the nation. Its ten half-minute advertising pauses sold at a premium afforded only by banks and finance companies.

No, the Pastor said, the reverse is true, the Giver is the Receiver – in his clear voice of a call across the abyss (its modulation steady on the advice of his production engineers, his eyes level and slightly to the right where the monitor finds the honesty of his expression) the Giver is the Receiver who, he paused (don't waver, they whisper into his tiny earphone), who does not Waver from the Paths of Selflessness, he said without breaking his rhythm.

A franchise, GranDoddie said, passing him a plate. Moral fast food.

GranDoddie turned to the Doctor. She was the only guest I ever saw invited twice. They had argued about feminism. She deplored it and was supported by mother. The Colonel had stayed quiet.

The Doctor swung an immense bust before her and strong buttocks behind, and strapped her trunk into corsetry so tightly she bulged at each end and swivelled on her axis like a weathercock.

She spoke loudly at mothers' clubs and was one of the sources that newsreporters sought for topical features on their women's pages. She championed dietary restraint, fecundity, and the woman's place as in the home. She was overweight, childless by choice, and took a hundred thousand dollars a year in her practice.

The expectations of gender, she said with her laugh of a raven, are inevitable.

I read you in the Saturday Supplement, GranDoddie said, your view that aggressiveness is fixed in the male chromosome? Yes, she used a softer voice than I thought her capable of, it is well substantiated, she said. Only men wage war.

That is patently wrong, GranDoddie said, in Vietnam it is not the case at all.

I was speaking, she said, of the white races. Her eyes floated flat as the yellow discs of a preying bird. Even at home, she told him, that war is waged between men.

I looked at the Colonel. He did not intervene.

Since the beginning of American involvement in Vietnam GranDoddie had written monthly to the newspapers. It was an unwinnable and immoral war, he said. His letters were ignored by the editor. GranDoddie was a veteran blooded in the slow mud of Flanders, another immoral war, and through only the fault of my frozen hip was I prevented, he cried, from holding a gun in the one just war of my memory, the war against fascism nineteen thirty-nine. These letters were not printed and neither were the next, though he claimed correspondence with Burchett and new certainties of defeat. The last of GranDoddie's letters lay on the editor's table at exactly the arrival of the Colonel's press-release scoffing, on behalf of the Returned Servicemen's League, at rumours that the scarred forests of Vietnam were being stripped by American poisons. GranDoddie's letters had described the curling of leaves to the twilight mists of low-flying bombers. The next issue of the *Glendale Guardian* carried each of their photographs, titled 'Father Against Son: The War At Home.'

Within a fortnight the American press had confirmed the use of chemical defoliants. GranDoddie pasted a copy of the *Washington Post* on his gate.

And your own war, the Doctor swooped on him, is ineffectual. You battle away at dinner-parties, though all you have to offer is, ha, satire at the expense of your guests. The Pastor joined her; the lampoon is easily hurled, he said, at the innocents.

GranDoddie's old eyesockets had become darker, though it may have been the moving afternoon.

Irony, he said; in an unjust society there is no humour more frequent than irony.

'Ironical,' the Solicitor told us as if we had not thought about it, 'that a man who knew so little about the worth of our society was so fortunate in exploiting its values.' He looked at the Colonel. 'Mr

Doddie has left to Elspeth a moderately worthy inheritance.'

The Colonel had thought of it often.

At the time public support for the war in Vietnam was being seen to splinter, public taste had begun to run against the Colonel's value of land. He had built his house on a block twice the size of GranDoddie's. Our land was sewered, kerbed, cleared and prominent. His was bushy and remote. Our house was cream-brick and triple-fronted. GranDoddie's was old.

Within three years of the purchase, our house was banal while GranDoddie's was coveted by the National Trust; our front rooms trembled to the roar of traffic as his eaves were host to the summer swallows. A square foot of his land was suddenly worth more than a square foot of ours.

To keep pace with it the Colonel built a patio and marked out the oblong of a swimming pool below, but saw he could not go on with it and kicked out the pegs. On his verandah GranDoddie sipped his beer and gazed over the creek.

The Solicitor waited for the Colonel to answer. 'It wouldn't be so bad' the Colonel said, 'if it were due to his better judgement.'

And now he is six months dead.

'Here. He is in this photograph.' The Solicitor reached across the desk and passed it to me, a framed press-reprint of a Remembrance Day march. Taking the salute, the Solicitor in his braided uniform of a Brigadier. And the Colonel beside him, their faces rigid. And in the crowd behind, the veterans too old to march, and GranDoddie, white hair and dark suit, across his breast the three rows of medal and coloured ribbon I remember from the Vietnam Moratorium marches – in the shambling cascade about him of jeans and sarongs and bicycles and headbands, of prams and briefcases, thirty-five abreast that took four hours to clear the wide pavements of Bourke Street alone, and I had found Doddie in the laughing midst of it, suited and medalled, striding out to the invisible band of the Colonel's parade-ground, volume with dignity, the pride of a faded military, an array of one, to the drum beat of another god and another country. He looked so silly.

And it is only now I realise that was the point.

Look again at the photograph.

There.

There is the scowl of a Glendale art dealer who lectures in Adult Education on the integrity of artistic form, and was sued by an abstract painter for slicing a single geometric canvas into four panels, selling them separately.

And there.

There is the orthopaedic surgeon who retired at forty-two to become a real-estate millionaire.

Who, I might ask him, did you use for bridging finance? Medibank?

And the Colonel's lips would pale.

Elspeth!

Ticket for Charity

When Charity Lord fell pregnant she told each of the six boys who were that month's quick loving, in turn, as they stumbled from the hotel.

Five of them pushed away, unbelieving or unworried, but Slow Billy gazed into the face that slumped on the left side where the calipers that had drawn her clumsy birth gave her the indelible and forlorn misery she buried willingly in any shoulder, and he nodded. He shoved the other five toward an empty room in the football club. Their arguments lasted for four hours.

To unlock them, someone suggested a Black Spot draw, and as Billy was the only one who had never heard of it, he owned up to the dot on his tuft of torn paper, just my luck he said while the others pulled theirs into tiny pieces, and Brownlow Billy was elected Best and Fairest, they laughed, on the first ballot.

He married her the next week.

Billy took Charity to live at his shack the night of the wedding, we can't afford a honeymoon. But she knew it was more than that: the carnival hypocrisy of a honeymoon with Charity Lord would raise grinning ironies he could not face.

Billy lived out in the Dust, under the rain-shadow; too dry for wheat, though it was said his father had tried it twice before he died, and Billy was too frightened to run sheep, even in the boom, in case they nipped out the light cover and the crimson topsoil blew away.

He could not risk a tractor. He grew vegetables for a living and watered them by hand. Billy could run flat-out with a bucket of water in each hand and his lumbering dash through the centreline of the football field was fearsome as a falling tree.

His vegetables were large as mutations, an unnatural product of the thousands of years the soil has lain without leaching, the government analyst said, but Billy couldn't work an area large enough to make money, even though he tilled behind an aged Clydesdale mare who wheezed the dust from her nostrils and coughed in the mornings like a consumptive.

Billy got up from the table. It was the first breakfast he had not cooked himself in eight years. He leaned over the back of Charity's shoulder and kissed her cheek and knew it was the first time any man had kissed her with tenderness. It's a day of firsts, he said, but did not explain it.

Wait a little she said, I'm coming too. I must have five months before it can do me any harm, and she looked into his slow face with eyes still wearing the gratitude of the white gown that had been her mother's.

He gave her a mattock and a four-gallon drum cut into a bucket and showed her where to work, while he led the mare to a one-acre plot damp enough, with dew from the crisp night, to plough. Charity finished by mid-day and his lunch was ready as he entered. He gave her a larger plot in the afternoon. By sundown his dinner was cooked. It took him two days to realise what was happening. She was working at a rate above half his pace, though he had the horse.

Billy left the mare and watched her. Charity bent down and up and down above the rows with the speed of dressmakers' scissors. Her hoe bit true at each stroke and the rows drew open behind her as steadily as a moving pencil. Not once did he see her pause to wipe the sweat from her face and her wasp-waist worked open and shut like a hinge he was frightened must wear out. Billy pulled her upright and she stood without swaying, but her face, twisted from the forced misfortune of her own hurried birth, ran the birthmark red of the soil. She was blind with her effort.

You can not do it like this, you cannot. It will harm, he looked at her stick thinness, both of you. I must, she said. I must make sure you are not the loser, and the lines in her slanted face were the years of her trying. He could not bear to hear the unmanageable burden of it. No, it is not like that, he said, there is nothing you owe, but she began to hoe again until he took it from her.

I won you, he shouted into her face, I won you in a raffle.

She stood still and looked at him unblinking. I know that, she said softly, you were so stupid you did not know it was rigged, but you went through with it. He watched the asymmetry in her smile. He had thought it ugly but it was wry; a mischievousness against the threat of innumerable defeats and the bravery of it flooded his cheeks. Come on, she said, and she took his hand to her gritty mouth, come up to the house and fuck with our love of the first time, and tomorrow we will work twice as hard.

In the morning they began a channel. Billy had hoped for three years he might find a way to irrigate the plots, reticulate to an old concrete tank from a soak under the hills, black with waterfowl at dusk, love, you couldn't believe the thousands, cutting the channel in a way that would not allow the dustbanks to blow in the warm winds.

Together they worked at it, he leading the mare as it dragged a single blade, Charity tilting the water kibble so the newly turned divots curled wet from the steel. The furrow was over half a mile long. They did it again deeper, and watched with envy as the white spring clouds rumbled over them to rain three miles further east and the wind underneath stirred the red dust to settle again on their boots. The third time, Billy trenched by hand, Charity sprayed from a stirrup pump and patted grey pellets of clover seed into the mud with her fingers. Her globular belly was tight and she had to squat to reach the ground.

The football coach sent a message from town. He was also the barman at the hotel. Pre-season training, he had scribbled on a cardboard drink-coaster, began Tuesday. Where were you? Billy didn't reply.

Billy thought Charity should stay in the house but she would not hear of it. Every five days he drove her into the Clinic and wanted to go in with her, but no, love, I want to see the district nurse alone. You go to the pub.

She watched him from inside the Clinic, through the fly-wire gauze. Billy stepped up onto the verandah without using the three planks of the stair, past the group that would contain her father, g'day, she's fine, over there at the Sister's, and then into the main bar.

Charity had stood in the shadow of that verandah often. Her arm about the corner-post. Dad, she called up, Mum says come home, but her father hated it and belted her after, with the drunken swipes of many more hatreds, so she squatted in the darkness under the rail and never said, and slept on the tin floor of his old panel-van, face down into the crook of her arm until he dragged her awake when they were home. That's why her face is out of shape, he said, she's always sleeping on it.

She had stood in the darkness of that verandah the night they were married. Her father had not come to the Chapel for the short ceremony. They found him later under the corner globe of the hotel verandah as if it were any other night. You ask him, she said, and I'll wait in the car, but she had not. She leaned her forehead against the red-gum foundation stump that was already smooth from the rubbing of her face as a child. Her father's voice was loud above her, but she could hear Billy behind the laughter of the other drinkers. It's a dowry he's asking, she heard her father roar, and, you've made your bed now lie with her. She pressed tight to the bole whose breadth had loved her for a decade, her father banged his glass onto the table, she's the best fuck in town, he said, everybody says so, and suddenly the scraping of bar-stools against the floorboards beside her head, the showing explosion of a glass tumbler promising a glitter the ear can only guess at. She ran to the car. Billy got in and slammed the door. They sat in silence for nearly a full minute. Your father said no. Billy had started the motor. Never mind, he'd said.

Billy drove them home. She thought of that night every time he drove her out of the town. Never mind, he'd said. She was lazy from the two weak shandies he had bought for her in the bar. Yes, love, Sister thinks everything is fine. Sister said, and Billy could hear her smile, that I'm in good shape.

For the next three weeks they watered the banks of the channel morning and night. Billy caught her crouching by the side of the dray holding her belly. No, she said, nothing wrong, it's not due for weeks yet. Her laugh was crooked but he could not tell if it was pain.

The morning was warm before it became light. Billy heard the excitement in her call and walked to the door. The banks of the trench had begun to burr with green. He hitched the watercarrier to the back of the dray and they began spraying. I want to lead the mare, Charity said, and Billy pumped the handle from the dray in slow piston strokes, building the pressure in the vessel until it was tight with air and the hosepipes were stiff with the effort of it. The rose gasped and the waters broke with a rush. The flow stopped abruptly, regained a trickle and dried. The dray had stopped.

Billy called to Charity to keep going and caught the tail of her cry under his last words.

Charity crouched beneath the mare's neck, briefs screwed about her ankles and skirt clenched to her knees, its threadbare denim stained with weak blood and hanging with mucus. She held back the heaving of her throat with teeth bared like death. Billy lifted and ran with her back to the shed, his footfalls exploded the hot dust and puffs of it hung in the still air behind him like brown shrubs.

She lay silently on the back seat of the car for the twenty miles to the hospital. He opened the door. She was holding the baby in her bloodied fingers and straining the cord tight as fencing wire. It was dead. Billy folded the hem of her skirt over it and began to lift her out. He saw it had been a boy.

As he stood up with her she gripped the back of his neck and pulled her slanted face into his with a fierceness that frightened him. Now that's over, she said, we can have a child of our own.

For the three weeks that Charity lay white on the hospital pillow Billy worked the plots. The day she came home her uneven eyes glistened, it's only a reaction to the glare, she said, but when she asked Billy to identify the rows of green shoots pushing out of the moist furrows, her laughter curled from her underlip in an animated questionmark. The new water had done more than increase their capacity by the hundredfold he guessed for her, it was painting their property green. Billy had planted trees. Their red dustbowl was becoming an oasis.

They gazed at it with a pride that filled his chest. He breathed it out, it's a place, he said, we can be proud of for the rest of our lives. Charity did not answer him immediately. I think, she said, we should talk about that.

Charity did not need the three months she had allowed for.

They walked from the concrete apron onto the grassed airstrip toward the aircraft. The concrete had been cracking in the heat of mid-day since Billy's father had laid it with a dole-team thirty years before. Billy stopped at the open hatch in the aircraft's belly. He wore a red and white checked suit Charity had chosen for him at the mercer's. He could not bear to wear the tie. Charity had arranged the sale of their property for a sum they both knew was their fortune. The new owner was a corporation of which they never remembered the name. It invested risk capital in ventures that offered the possibility of immense returns and was to convert the plots into a feeding complex to fatten lambs for the new markets of the moslem east.

Its caterpillar-tracked machinery began to arrive before dawn that morning with the continuous roar of a busy aircraft carrier. Billy had watched the invaders with amazement. They're mad, he said.

Charity drew him toward the aircraft. She wore white gloves and held both their tickets in her hand. A new breeze twitched the grass about his feet, a northerly, he said, it'll all be gone by morning.

Melodrama for a Plastic Heroine

He begins to puff before beginning to climb the hill. At the intersection, he waits for company before he dares to cross. He cannot keep up with the city shoppers and with businessmen on important errands, and fans himself with the lapel of his jacket. The jacket and the trousers have once belonged to different suits. His hat fits him so poorly that he holds it to the top of his head with a hand. The bashful flesh of his ankles is not covered by socks. The cuffs on his trousers have grown obese over ten or twelve years of tapering fashions and twirl about heavily as if they had really hoped, in adolescence, to be auditioned as skirts for leggy chorus girls.

The scrap he holds so tightly was once part of a magazine page. He squints at the printing on it. The item he needs to check seems to have become minuscule since he last looked at it. By the time he again looks up, he has wandered to a halt.

There is now a gap in his understanding of where he is, but he seems in no hurry to repair it. He is happiest when the events which make up his day are episodic.

He has come to a brightly lit shop-front.

Those about him do not glance at this shop. They ignore it more pointedly than if it were an empty lot. Its window has been painted out with white, and bordered with peristaltic rows of theatrical globes. Its number, inscribed over the doorway in accordance with

municipal regulation, is 666. This has been transcribed on the
window, in accordance with advertising practice, as Sex-Sex-Sex.

He catches himself staring too long through the open door. With
the air of one who must have been day-dreaming, he turns sharply
away. He walks on quickly. He is in a hurry to be somewhere else
altogether.

Wait. If we stay here for little longer than it might take for a tubby
man who is capable only of oblique steps to walk to the next corner,
and to stop as if he had lost his way, and to turn himself resolutely
about for the opposite direction, we will see him again.

On the way back, he has picked up an air of bewilderment. The
number inscribed over the door of this shop seems to be the same as
the number on his scrap of paper, but it would be clear to anyone
who glanced at him that he cannot believe he has business at such an
address.

He shrugs into a mantle of resignation. He dabs his mouth against
the threat of a slight but disturbing cough. Somehow this also
necessitates turning up his collar and lowering the brim of his hat.

Footfalls heavily ornamented with dignity carry him inside.

The proprietress sits behind the counter. Her eyeglasses are thick and
she has hair piled into a bun on the top of her head. She is reading a
book and is not anxious to put it down.

His cough does not disrupt her concentration. He looks around,
but the item he seeks is evidently nowhere about. His gaze does not
wander far, for there are things on the walls and in display boxes on
which he does not wish his eyes to rest. When the woman looks up,
he is clearly her second priority.

He is not yet able to trust his voice. Exertion, and the anxieties of
deceit, have left him breathless. He draws a small shape in the air, but
his fingers are so uncomfortable about it that she does not understand
them.

He passes her his scrap of paper. The advertisement on it is familiar
to her. She closes her book loudly against the counter and makes
toward a doorway at the back of the shop. He has gathered together
enough presence of mind to follow. She leads him through, as he tries

to steady his breathing, and she turns on the light.

Immediately his impression is of a blunder.

The cubicle resembles a cramped room back-stage in a night-club. It is crowded with young women, naked, and as glossy as if they were still wet from the shower. That their bodies are lifeless in any biological sense, and that their personalities have been moulded only by the passion of heat on plastic film, is not, on the instant, important. The light has caught them all in poses of mid-movement. Their gazes are still and evasive.

There is only one at whom he can look without a migraine of embarrassment, a brunette standing at the back. It is not so taut, not so hostile, as the rest.

Leaning into the crowd, he takes the brunette by the arm. But concern for his own dignity has made him clumsy. He nudges others. A red-head bumps about angrily. It seems courteous that he take off his hat.

He lays his money on the counter. He stands his doll beside it. The woman seems slow to understand what he is doing.

'You can't take one outside like that,' she says.

For the first time he realises she is wrapping a carton. He is horrified that it is for him. He hugs his own doll closer.

Its gaze is now shy but expectant. He recognises the instant as decisive, and his decision is both noble and cavalier. With an arm about her waist, he lifts his damsel clear of the floor and canters for the door.

He runs, holding his hat on with the other hand, directly on to the roadway.

Cars stampede around them. His jacket floats like a cape. The cars bellow. He switches directions rapidly to confuse them. He is proud of his quick thinking. The last few yards form a declension of full-tilts, and he hurdles the kerb in a single bound.

Slowly they climb the three dark flights of his tenement. They rest. The doll leans against the wall. He opens a door with his key. He

turns to gather her up. She lies, now, full length across his arms.
He carries her over the threshold.

This room is a bed-sitter. Its window looks out over the street.
Pinned to the walls are old enlargements of publicity photographs.
They show actors in costumes of nineteenth-century London. On the
plaster above them hang posters advertising *The Beggar-Girl's
Wedding*, *The Worst Woman In London*, and *Pure As The Driven Snow*.

A framed portrait hangs at the end of the room. It shows a strident
and theatrical woman in her forties. Her voice is in full flight.
Against the wall underneath it stands a wheelchair. The wheels and
frame are of richly polished mahogany. Lacquer on the armrests has
been worn away.

The doll stands beside his wardrobe. Its open door covers her from
shoulder to knee like a dressing-cubicle. He rummages about for a
slip, a skirt, and a blouse. These he hangs over the door. He discounts
an absurd inclination to tell her that they had belonged to his
Mother.

He has difficulty finding enough shoes to make a matching pair.
'These were Mother's,' he says.

The doll is sitting on the couch. She is almost fully dressed, although
he has not quite finished buttoning the front of her blouse. It is not
easy. He does it with his gaze averted, and is having trouble fitting
her all in. The word *Bubbles* bursts into his mind. He is excited at
having thought of so daring a love-name for her. The words *daring*
and *manliness* seem to him, for the moment, to have much in
common.

But, when he utters her name aloud for the first time, he watches
her slyly for the tremor of an unfavourable reaction.

He stands her in front of the mirror. Her blouse narrows daintily to
the waist and the skirt falls fluently to the ankle. The skirt carries a
pattern of vermilion daisies on a white field, appropriate for a
coming-out dance at a country hall, although in fact it was once part
of the wardrobe for the production of *The Peasant's Lovely Daughter*.

The sight fills him with a pride in her which he thinks of as selfless affection. He allows her to face her reflection alone.

It does not confuse him that he feels also an expectation of gratitude.

'Now,' he says, 'I'm going to take you out to dinner.'

The restaurant is evidently either Spanish or Italian. Their table is too large for two, it is set with a red-checked cloth, there is a basket of chunky bread, and the music is too loud. They have not yet eaten, for the cutlery is undisturbed, but the wine bottle is half empty.

He holds a cigarette between thumb and forefinger in a manner he thinks appropriate in a restaurant. Sometime, he has brushed most of the ash from his lap. Small-talk has never come easily to him, so he hums, now, to a few bars of the music. He recognises the tune: Up, up and away, In my beautiful balloon.

'Shall we consider this,' he says, 'as our song?'

They dance in front of their table. His ballroom stance is a pose which also parodies a bout of flatulence. They perform a few steps of fox-trot. The reverse he executes is not steady, but he handles it all with a vision of his own grace. The next tune is livelier. He confuses his fox-trot with jive. He reels her out and in, rocks her from one hip to the other. His ankles flash. He has never felt so sure-footed. She leans backward until her head sweeps close to the floor. He judges her height with a quick eye. He can leap that high. The Leap was a competition step popular in the forties. His movement resembles the action which, if the altitude were different, high-jumpers call The Roll.

His foot lands squarely, but somehow the floor has tilted in the meantime. Bubbles is not strong enough to hold him. She buckles. As tangled and disjointed as unstrung marionettes, they topple toward the floor.

That she followed his every lead was a compliment he would have paid her, if they were not already on his way down.

There is, of course, no restaurant; only devices of the solitary.

The table, with its red-checked cloth and chunky bread, is in the centre of his room. Other furniture stands where he has pushed it against the walls. His phonograph has come to the end of the track and lifts off with a snap.

He is able to get up only as far as onto his knees before he finds that something is wrong. Bubbles' arm has fallen listlessly onto the floor. Somewhere there is also a faint sound of hissing. He listens. He feels across her shoulders, and lower, over her torso. His hands are pale and without lewdness. With a finger, he stops the hissing. The rupture is further down than he can bring himself to look.

He carries her to the bed. Her head is motionless on the pillow. It seems to him that her face is sagging. He puts an ear to her mouth. Any ghost of her breath is beyond his hearing.

The room fills with the sound of knocking on his door. He makes no move. He knows who this is. The voice from behind his door is a woman's.

'Church Welfare,' she says. The tone is peremptory.

He thinks always of her as Mrs Welfare. He is not sure if he has ever addressed the title to her. On this day in the week she inspects his head for lice and the skin on his cheeks for signs of vitamin deficiencies. She inspects the room, and his reasons for not going to Church. He remembers her breath as harsh.

'I know you are there,' she says. Her voice is now too edgy for him to risk a sound.

The building in which the room is belongs to the Church. He feels justified in thinking of Mrs Welfare as his landlord's bailiff.

'I'll be back,' she says. 'Don't you worry.'

He turns warily back to the bed.

Arranged in neat conformation on the bedside table are strips of adhesive tape, a towel, a bundle of plastic bags, scissors. He massages his hands. His fingers stand stiffly out. He scrutinises them. They stare back, shivering with nystagmus. He remembers an old gibe of his mother's: that he faints at the sight of blood.

The implements on the dresser lie now in a disarray of recent use.

A white sheet covers Bubbles to the chin. He is holding his vigil over her. He cannot remember how long he has been standing here. Fading blood stains the tips of his fingers. Somehow, he has cut his thumb. There is a lighted candle at the bedside. Its flame is thin. His face swims quietly with tears.

The theatrical photographs on the walls have become noisier than the movement of his own thoughts. The figures in them shuffle and murmur. The tableaux change. The captions are not as he remembered them.

Caption: *Mother And Father.*
Scene: Inside the hall of a country town. Of its thirty rows of seats, the audience fills only the first eight. The acoustics are such that the loudest sound in the hall is the fidgeting of shoes. The folk in them have each paid five shillings to see this performance of *Her Father's Guilty Secret*. The principal players are husband-and-wife team Amelia and Archibald Bliss. Gestetnered programme notes show that Archibald Bliss has, so far, handsomely saved the swooning Amelia from one thousand eight hundred fates worse than death and, together, they have escaped disaster in two thousand and forty nicks of time.

This is the final act. A tubby and serious boy, whose features are familiar to us, displays a title-board to the audience. It reads: *A New Life*. He runs off. At centre stage, Archibald, in top-hat and kneeling on the hem of his cape, is pleading forgiveness from Amelia. She does not appear, tonight, as ready to grant it as the script requires. Her face might be as white from anger as from purity, for, during the last costume-change, Archibald has told her of his passion for an adagio dancer at the Trocadero.

When the curtain comes down, this audience will applaud, for less than a half-minute, the last of the Bliss Family's Travelling Melodramas.

Caption: *Twelve Identical Years.*
  Scene: Inside his bed-sitter. This scene is familiar to him
            although he has not seen it so clearly from this
            direction before. He stands behind his Mother. Amelia
            has, since Archibald ran off, taken to a wheelchair. Her
            need for it does not seem to be physiological. She sits
            gazing through the window. Her most frequent
            statement is: Look, that world is for husband-and-wife
            acts.

Caption: *A Mother's Sacrifice.*
  Scene: Inside the bed-sitter. A day in mid-week (since he
            remembers waking to the sound of morning traffic).
            The wheelchair is empty. His Mother could not be far.
            But a message is written on the mirror: *Gone out to die
            in the snow.* The temperature is already thirty degrees
            Celsius and the summer solstice is not long past. She
            has taken their savings and small change from a vase on
            the dresser. His watch is gone.

Caption: *Is Life Worth Living?*
  Scene: His clothes are one year more threadbare. He now lives
            on handouts. His palms are deeply lined, for he cleans
            the stairs and the light-well to work out the rent. He
            hangs his mop upside down under the stairs. It is the
            heavy gesture of one who has done this for the last
            time. His face is resolute.

Caption: *The Curtain Falls.*
  Finale: He sits beneath the portrait of his Mother. He has
            chosen her wheelchair in which to drain away his life.
            He is attempting to score his wrist with a knife. But
            control of the blade is beyond him. He needs both his
            hands around the handle to keep the knife from
            shaking.

Finale (2): He stands on the roof. His eyes are tightly shut. The drop to the pavement would be more than sufficient to expunge him quickly. His face has taken on the dappled complexion of seasickness, and he is unable to move his feet. He is so affected by vertigo that he cannot edge closely enough to the parapet to leap.

Finale (3): He sits over his dinner. It is yet untouched. He normally thinks of himself as an enthusiastic eater. But the thought of the ratsbane he has cooked into it has caused him to lose his appetite.

There is no Finale (4).

The heroine who was to have played that tender but triumphant scene with him lies on his bed. His predicament is now, as it is always, a measure of his own capacity for gracelessness. In their posters on the wall, the actors and the bit-players have resumed their poses. He cannot see them clearly from where he stands, but imagines that their expressions reflect pity and shame. In her portrait at the end of the room, his Mother's voice has resumed that ceaseless note which is too high for the human ear.

He turns back to Bubbles and leans over her. He touches her cheek with his own. He does not hold it there long, for gestures of affection embarrass him. Her face is now wet with his sorrow.

There is something about this which unsettles him. He lifts her hand. There is here, if not response, at least a resilience he was not expecting. Her shoulder has substance. Her thigh is round.

His breath is still in her.

Bubbles is recuperating.

She now sits in the wheelchair with a blanket over her lap. The gas fire is alight. Weak tea is on the small table. He sits on a chair drawn up beside her, flipping the pages of a brochure. Its illustrations are large and glossy. They are the advertisements of Sepulchral Masons.

Finale (4) is again on-line.

Knocking sounds on his door. He says nothing. He puts a finger over Bubbles' lips. The knocking sounds again. Mrs Welfare's voice is determined.

'I am not going away.'

He turns the wheelchair so that its back is toward the door, and quietly crosses the room. He opens the door, but the gap it makes is ungenerous. This is not an invitation to enter.

He mimes the actions of a weightlifter, although the power of his biceps does not make it past the weight of cloth in his jacket. He speaks the caption aloud:

'A Picture of Health and Strength.'

'Don't be fatuous,' she says, and pushes her way inside.

Here is a woman used to doing as she wishes. Her Derby is imperiously straight. The brass tip of her ebony cane never touches the floor. She wears a dark cape, falling to the heel. The width of her shoulders suggests that she might originally have been designed to be tall.

She catches sight of the figure in the wheelchair.

'Has your Mother come home, Mr Bliss?'

He hopes to block her way.

'A Sick Friend,' he says. 'A Friend in Need. A Stitch in Time.'

'A Lodger,' says Mrs Welfare. 'You are not permitted a lodger.'

And she strides past to confront the lodger.

In front of the wheelchair, Mrs Welfare is unable to speak.

Her gaze is fixed on the doll's mouth. Since that mouth is ever partly open and as soft and round as a discreet Oh, he has always thought of it as expressing a delicate surprise.

Mrs Welfare's mouth expresses a surprise of quite a different nature.

'An Honourable Union,' he quickly says.

Mrs Welfare is unmoved. Clearly, he has not made himself understood. It will require the grace of a full sentence to convey to her that this is not as sordid as she thinks.

He takes the doll's hand in his own.

'We are engaged to be married,' he says.

Mrs Welfare turns again at the door. Her voice is cramped with disgust. Her cassock swirls.

'Take that sinful effigy out of here. Or out you go.'

She disappears down the stairs in a cascade of footsteps.

He remembers a caption, but cannot recall the play in which he displayed it.

Bell, Book, and Candle.

The door is bolted.

The window is closed. A rolled towel huddles in the space under the door. The room is still, but for the phonograph's precise addiction to 0.5 rotations in each second which ticks past. This is a little slow by recording standards, so the song it plays has greater melancholy than when Porgy sang to his Bess in performance:

It's a long way,
But you'll be there
To take my hand.

Only in the pause between verses can a grimy and monotonous gust of escaping gas be heard blowing from the fireplace.

Bubbles lies on the floor. She wears a white gown which was once the succinct costume for the blameless heroine of *Betrothed & Betrayed*. Her veil does not match that gown, for it was once the dusty voile fringing this window.

He lies beside her, wearing, now, a darker jacket, but perhaps he has merely brushed the other. His shirt-collar is fastened although he has no tie, and the grey legs of his trousers have been tugged down to the ankles. Some time, he has taken pains to blacken the soles of his shoes. He is holding her hand.

The song ends.

The pick-up has run to the end of the record, but it sticks in the tail-groove. Kss. Kss. He opens an eye. Kss. He closes it again.

He will wait it out.

There is no movement from either of them.

The pick-up lifts from the disc. Its motion is worn and groggy. The hissing of gas is now the only sound in the room. It, too, has begun to undulate. Its breathing flutters, and staggers on. But it is uncertain.

He has again opened an eye. Without otherwise moving his body, his hand gropes for the fire-side plumbing. The box over which his fingers now hover is a coin-operated gas regulator.

The gas fades. He pats his pockets, and sits up as though better to see that the hearth is empty.

A more ill-humoured man might then have reflected on the way of a world which prevents the poor from asphyxiating themselves cheaply. But resentfulness is not in his nature. He holds his head in his hands. He is merely rueful that he has selected only the correct number of coins to purchase himself a headache.

They stand together at the open window. Her head is thrown back and the veil lifts lightly to the breeze. It surprises him that the air of so crowded a city can smell sweet.

Already he has begun to share blame equally between them, for his thought now is: We must have been out of our minds.

The footpath below has become busy with people.

This is the time, late in the day, when the flows are strong and deliberate, and will wash into queues at bus terminals and railway stations. The sun is out of sight. Buildings are in shade like the shadows of cliffs. The light between them is blue. Flights of white gulls glide low. The tide of the city has turned.

The people he watches can see little of this. Men with stiff lapels to their jackets, and women whose parcels are awkward, and teenagers with surer footfalls and vinyl cases ribbed with the outlines of games racquets, all are hurried and purposeful. For the first time it strikes him as curious, rather than frightening, that the habitual expression of the human face is passionless. The duration of contact one with another, the frown, the nod, the smile, is fleeting and minimal. In this part of town most will be office-workers. Their affinities with information systems, word processors and data programmes are varied and intricate. Their affinities with each other are elemental and intermittent. It is as if they have withdrawn to a binary system of human response.

A man could pass among them unnoticed, at times like these.

The light of decision is again in his eye. Had he been able to see it, he might think it a cruel light.

He drops Bubbles into the wheelchair. There is a kit-bag in the wardrobe. It is so old that, when he dusts it off, flakes of leather come away. He empties a drawer. Socks, shirts, underwear. A raincoat. And – all without looking up at her, for this has got to be a clean break – he sweeps into it the mis-matched cufflinks, the gummy combs, and the dusty nick-nacks that the top of a dresser collects over twelve years, and snaps the bag shut.

But he is unable to leave her so abruptly.

He finds the blanket to drape over her lap. At the phonograph, he reloads the spindle and switches it on. Before he can reach the door the pick-up begins to play.

I loves you Porgy . . .

He knows, now, the chill felt by a deserting spouse.

On the footpath he holds his hat to his head with a hand. He is unused to being jostled. His tubby gait seems to take up more room than that to which he is evidently entitled. His bag bumps nervously. His coat-tail twitches about. With effort, he is almost successful in appearing as preoccupied as anyone. But the song has got him. It hums in his head.

I loves you, Porgy . . .

He passes the window display of a fashion boutique. At first glance it seems crowded, but these are plaster figures, well-dressed and haughty. He looks quickly away. He feels the gaze of the mannequins on him. His ears burn.

The song, for all he knows, plays on. Perhaps her head is now downcast. Has the veil fallen over her face?

The door bursts open.

He wheels her chair around. That her eyes have brightened, and that she sits now eagerly upright, he does not attribute to the weight of his kit-bag on her lap.

The footpath seems busier still. This day is drawing to a close for so many people. The conduits along which they flow will dim the city and brighten the suburbs. He imagines them being then deflated, one by one, and fed into narrow drawers or hung in closets until breakfast-time.

He pushes fast enough to match the consensus of velocity. They have now made a place for themselves in this crowd. He has never felt so carefree. They have reached the top of the hill and crossed the road before he realises that the effort has cost him no discomfort at all.

Here, then, is the shop-window lit by globes he thinks of as footlights, with its title Sex-Sex-Sex. The woman sitting behind the counter watches the crowd rolling past her open door. Perhaps she has finished her book. There is no need to pause before her more than briefly, and now he pushes on. This small event has made him smile, for it has occurred to him that her spectacles are the shape which cartoonists draw to represent astonishment.

And here is a vendor selling wind-up toys and balloons and dizzy windmills from a barrow. He pays for two balloons.

They crowd about and make his choosing difficult. He takes time to decide on a red and a blue. Their cheeks seem to him chubby and irrepressible, and they tug, now, at his hand with the campaigning impatience of small children. He wheels them all away, and they set off for the far side of the hill.

For this was once the invariable direction of Bliss family outings, down to the wharves and the docks, to liners fresh from Durban and traders sweaty from the doldrums and freighters stencilled with the names of smoky ports in the Baltic, each of them evidence of the boundlessness available to the human fantasy.

Whoring Around

Prologue

More and more we lunched at his tennis club. He had recently become its Honorary Treasurer. I remember an afternoon, with the washed blues and faint yellows of early winter, when we ate on the terrace. The stonework was damp where the sun had not touched it. The other tables were empty, so it was early in the week.

The grounds were set in a natural bowl. Although the city centre must have been less than a mile away, we looked over lawn courts, rose walks and a gazebo as displaced and untimely as a country club from the thirties. A groundsman began to tie together a new court with white strings and wooden pegs. On a slope below the gravelled driveway, a gardener lifted dripping squares of turf to clear a collapsed drain which was, Humphrey told me, the single most disturbing item of unplanned expenditure facing the current year.

One court was in use. The two women were not playing well, and the sound of the ball was dissonant and irregular, but they laughed with the fun of it and the white pleating in their short skirts fluttered in the cold sunlight. The player at the closer end was younger than I had first noticed, a girl perhaps not yet eighteen. Her splendid hair swept about as she hit the ball.

The texture of the game suddenly roughened.

The older woman struck more firmly and shot often to the limit of the girl's reach as though she had become aware we were watching.

Her feet were light and her arm swung with the loaded memory of a once commanding player. Her hairstyle held fast in the cumulus fashion of that season, but the alpine tan on her arms and throat began to glisten and her breath misted at each sudden effort.

The girl fell back to the baseline. She mis-hit into the ground and high into the air. Her lucky shots were pointless and confused. Finally, she held up her hand and play stopped. As they walked together to the dressing-rooms the girl chattered incessantly and her laughter was careful.

I was glad that nasty little display had ended, but Humphrey must have been admiring the older woman throughout. He was smiling. Quality tells, he said.

I do not remember what pieces of his stories Humphrey told me then. He always told them readily and I had heard many before. But I know that when he began I thought his laughter, too, was careful.

During his first pauses we watched the groundsman stalk the periphery of his new court, pushing a paint-roller shaped like a broom, so he seemed to be sweeping away an opaque layer to expose the bright and indelible design he knew was already there.

Blowing It

Humphrey stood on the footpath outside the bar, pressed against the cardinal and gold panels by the troubled volumes of Chinese, and leaning away from them as if he were falling off some tireless production line of human figures. An overhead neon sign flashed between English and Chinese to the rhythm of a quick heartbeat and shadowed his jawline as though he were clenching his teeth.

The entrance became a stairwell. Humphrey brushed the front of his suit with his hands. The bottom stairs darkened and the passageway opened into a larger room before he noticed the change.

He could see one bar only. It was circular and Humphrey could make out six, perhaps eight drinkers around it. He could not see a bar-girl until he was close enough to slide onto a stool.

She was naked, but for a scarf printed with a red hibiscus bloom in her lap, and she lay on a couch. Her body lit the drinkers' faces like a flame; it was the only source of light. She lifted an arm and the faces flared and flickered. The bar held her in a crucible and from its edges a canopy of cigarette smoke drifted to a lamp set into the ceiling.

Her head rolled to face him, the flat cheeks glittering like gilded gift paper, the cut-out eyes wide and empty. She smelled of camphorwood incense. She swung her legs to the floor and sat upright, as light as a marionette. But tall, Humphrey thought, for a Chinese. She was oiled. Humphrey pulled his hands from the bar as if he had been irreverent. The girl leaned forward; her breasts were barely fuller than a boy's. But she was not so young, maybe, you can't tell with Asians. The virgins, especially, all look young. He took the printed drink list from her. Thank you, he began, but she had dropped from his sight and he could hear the changing of cassettes in a console under the bar. He could not read the list easily. Poor light rather than too much wine at dinner, I haven't had that much.

He heard laughter and smoke wavered like a veil. Humphrey looked at the other drinkers. None was Chinese. An American, chunky as an amateur wrestler and wearing a university T-shirt, held the hand of one English-woman and talked to another. A merchant seaman chanted a Glasgow football dirge in a slow rumble, chin hard against his chest as if fighting wind, so drunk he could not lift his full glass from the bar. A Japanese sat opposite in business shirt and tie but without a suit-coat, sharpening his cigarette on the ashtray like the tip of a pencil. Humphrey picked up a match folder and opened it. A pair of cardboard breasts flopped out, Boob's Bar Kowloon. He put them back.

Thank you, he said, I'll have a scotch, and again when she had poured, thank you, and as she slid the glass toward him on a coaster shaped like a pair of heavy watermelons, thank you very much, he said. She gave not the slightest sign of interest.

Humphrey felt the effects of the whisky quickly. Its vapours filled his chest with a heated perfume and his eyes moistened. He was not a heavy drinker by the standards he knew, not practised, not by his father's measure. Nor by his wife's. Mimi said it often: some men drink, she put it, easily. He preferred to drink at home, or at the tennis club where he was then known as a good fourth, and he feared the house parties given by Mimi's friends largely because he could not break into the circular conversations of the husbands, through their bumping guffaws, Mimi, I can't burrow down between their legs and heave up into the topic like a half-blind mole, it's not me. He sat with the women, do you mind, until their smiles drifted away in the diffident swirls of his interjections and she had to take him home.

Every night he worked in the study. You won't get the job, Mimi told him. Humphrey did not answer her. He kept working. She told him again when she got home from the theatre. She was not surprised to find him still working. The paper work made five neat piles on the desk. Before they were married, she now told even her lunchtime friends, she had mistaken his diligence for ambition. Not a chance, she told him.

But he did. Humphrey set up the structure of the Fossil Extracts Conference in less than two months. He was appointed to do it, you were wrong Mimi, he said without bile for his stomach had been scoured by twenty years of their resentments, I have been assigned until further notice. His employer was one of ten member companies to the agreement, to the Conference, as they called it. Each of those companies converted fossil deposits into a convenient form for processing into plastics or fuels or packaging materials and sold the product to their own subsidiaries or to each other. The plants and animals that had laid down their lives to bubble into gastric slime had lived three hundred million years before, dying mindlessly in geomantic layers for heat and pressure to harden for the benefit of posterity. Those companies saw themselves as that posterity and benefited. But the companies multiplied, Mimi, listen to me and you will understand it, multiplied according to laws of available sustenance older than the vulcanised moors they dug. The answer was a cartel.

Think of it, Mimi, a cartel, and Humphrey began from scratch, he told her, it's never been done like this before, on this scale. The Heads of Agreement were slim by comparison, but the ancillary contracts, the documentation, would fill half a dark room, memoranda and articles drawn and submitted and drawn again, Whereas the Parties Desire, by ten firms of lawyers, their names alone take up a page and a half, working in teams around the clock in shirtsleeves like poker players on a streak, that's why I'm late, and lobbying for government sanction, delicate but we can, he told us over lunch, look to favourable consideration, he is a source close to the Minister, what's good for the nation, though the Party contribution is a hundred grand more than we budgeted, but we should hear by Tuesday, by Friday he thinks, when it's all done, Mimi, we'll spend a few days at the coast, don't bother she said, and Humphrey designed a staff structure stronger than a family tree but without, the Board laughed with him, the dead wood, and the recommendations are in, working capital, and lines of credit established in Dollars and Yen and Deutschmark, en demande, a phonecall and it's there.

There.

The effort had drained Humphrey of his reserve. He was too tired to cover the childishness of his anticipation. I'll be going to Japan, Mimi, as head of the Conference. Hong Kong and Japan first, Europe later.

No chance, she said.

We want you to go to Japan, they told him. The sheets of his recommendations were strewn the length of the Boardroom table, a crazy-path, Mimi, from the bottom to the top, you were wrong.

To Japan, they paused, as assistant to Butcher. Butcher of Mincorp, they told me, he will lead you. I know him, Humphrey said, a good choice, and closed the panelled door quietly as he left.

How can you hold up your head, she said, you're as timid as a bird. You're being screwed as usual. Anger hardened in his throat like a growth. I can do that too, all expense account, screw my prick off.

Screwing it on is the problem, she turned toward her dressing-room, you've forgotten where you put it. Humphrey sat on the bed.

So the march to destroy the spectre of competition begins, he called after her, not to the hymns of uniting workers, but to the rattling chains of capital. Humphrey pulled off his shoes. Think of it, Mimi, and as he thought of it, Humphrey knew the lapping tide of his laughter had begun to turn after a thirty-year ebb.

Humphrey's glass was again empty. He did not know how many he had drained. The girl reached from the couch to the console, and Humphrey pushed his glass forward but she turned the volume louder and lay back, tapping her slicked belly to the rubber-ball syncopations of its catchy beat as if her skin had been tensioned.

She was the most beautiful object he had ever seen, a perfection that struck him as intensely inhuman. It reached beyond mood or character, as vacantly exquisite as a rich sarcophagus. Reaching beyond morality and inhibition; yet without prerogative or authority. She was entirely servile, an item of male plunder.

It excited him and he quickly confused this with manhood. She would do anything I want, he thought, that is what she is for. Anything at all.

This is a demesne some men are born to and others assume or appropriate; the Brothers who had taught him and the priests who married and absolved him must have known it though it was never directly spoken, and merely hinted in the displays of Asian and Roman and Egyptian antiquity to which Mimi had dragged him with the impatience of a schoolmistress through the interminable makeshift labyrinths of exhibition galleries, past the eyes of regents and their sacrificed concubines scaled with the ancient mail of their imperishable currency, past tribunes and their maidens in terracotta held together only by the diminishing humidity of an age, past deathmasks carved in pairs by whittlers who were somehow longer dead than the ageless cry they continue to immortalise, you do not understand it Mimi, but she would not listen; even he had not seen what they were really showing him, that each was master by merely acts of will; he understood it only at this very instant and the power of it made him sit upright, though he knew his straightening back was a metaphor for the pitiless hardening of his virility.

I will talk to her. But as he thought of it, scraps of adolescent failure rustled in his memory like old photographs. He fingered his gold lighter, I might give it to her, a present to inflame your admirers. Mimi had given it to him on their wedding anniversary the year before. The case held a roughly grained texture and felt heavy in the hand. He had seen it previously in the richly draped centrecase of a boutique at the corner of their street and had rejected the idea of it as a gift for her. An excess of expenditure over imagination, Mimi.

Three men now drank together on the opposite side of the bar. He had not seen them enter. She will light their cigarettes with an insolent snap but otherwise ignore them. The merchantman from Glasgow still sat alone, his mallet chin slumped onto the knitted bulk of his navy chest. He seemed to focus on her but could not hold it. He pressed his glass to his chest with both hands. Humphrey waited for it to shatter. The sailor stood as the stool tumbled slowly to the floor. His jowls began to work but their slabs made the stiff articulations of a ventriloquist's dummy. He thought he was singing. Humphrey's fingers tightened on the edge of the bar but the sailor made for the door in his fitful waltz to a heaving sea, the glass dropped and his hands reached for a steel railing. That seaman had, she will tell me in her whisper of a sad confidant, sat at her bar for the last five nights, pouring whisky into his hard mouth as mechanically as filling a boiler, chanting the slow homesick songs of Scotland. His ship, she will say it pressing the tips of my fingers, his ship steamed for home at five this morning.

His glass was again full. How many times might she have served it with such humility that no ripple of it reached him? Perhaps he had simply not drunk the last.

She sat facing the Japanese. Their conversation was solemn. She sat straight as a schoolgirl and the round of her buttocks gleamed the colour of waxed oranges. She would do anything I want, it is the way she lives, her vocation. How much will it cost? No matter, we can go to your hotel-room and relax, she will say. The money is little, enough to purchase the evening she would lose for her boss, she will tell me, to pay for another in her place. His gambling debts in Macao do not allow him to be more generous. I pull a lump of crushed notes from my pocket. The money is nothing. Her parents are two years dead. The rent of her high concrete room and its balcony flapping with gay laundry is a pittance. A top-coat she has on order for a month now, she tells me, is almost ready, the tailor is her uncle but he needs forty-two dollars for the material. A nice-girl's coat, she says, I look respectful, I must be well dressed to keep my job.

Humphrey felt a sudden glare from her body on his cheek. She was turning toward him. Her face was as expressionless as beaten foil. She was her own reflected image. His breath caught in his chest as though he had been running and he could see her mouth move but he could hear nothing.

I will have her.

I will slip the first of my words lightly about her shoulder, almost to touch the swayed back of her doll-smooth neck, watching the eyelids wisp lower to hide her interest, lilting my vowels over the faintest tip of worldly conceit, hold the conversation momentarily still, a neutrality offering the opportunity of acquiescence by hesitation and then by default, hiding the impetus of a later excitement softly under the swelling puberty of her breast until she is held by the feather-lightness of its breath on her skin, fluttering down the tightening of her belly, an insistence pressed against the bowl of her childish buttock, knowing the slackening of her open lips is a lust of which she is not now ashamed, and we grasp at it, both, into a dancing, hip-jerking abandon, thrusting under the rose-tinctured moisture of it and she can not close her flooding eyes against the virgin terror of its ruthless meaning, gripped with an urgency that is no longer cruel, dashed against each other by an overwhelming truth deep-pouring from me with the sudden essence of a bursting sac, an explosion, concussive and blinding, tears running into my salty cry with the slow memory of pain, revolving to the sweeter crux of pity, from which I can no longer move.

Mother of God.

I'm drunker than I thought, he said aloud, and wiped his cheek.

Well, she said, you coming to life now, time enough. Buy me a drink this time?

No.

He could answer her only with difficulty and his voice was dead. No, I need some rest, he said, and he knew his cheeks were grey and his eyes sagged. Your eyes dribble with fatigue like an exhausted spaniel, Mimi told him, no stamina at all. He slid off the stool and looked again at the girl's face. The head was unnaturally round and had the vacant malevolence of a halloween mask. He stared at her breasts, they were mean and without promise of motherhood, and he felt disgust bubble in his throat like an acid.

His lump of crushed notes lay on the bar. He counted some of it

out: ten, twenty, thirty, forty, forty-two. There, he said as she drew
away from it, that's for your coat.

He stumbled from the doorway into the pedestrian stream. The
light was harsh. The current sucked him past the shopfronts. Some
were still open. Cab-horns sounded from a roadway he couldn't see;
grey water ran the gutter and splashed the pavement although it had
not been raining. His eyes closed out the strobed glare from display
windows beaded with lightbulbs. The force of movement around him
stopped at an intersection. He stood in a wide queue as police
directed traffic on both sides of nine workers excavating a floodlit
trench in the centre of the road. Most of the pick-workers were
women. They wore the black work-singlets of men and chipped at the
bitumen crust without glancing up at the traffic.

Humphrey joined the group waiting to cross. It bulged over the
kerbline. He was pushed forward and across the road, closely behind
three women in wide-bottomed trousers and short canvas jackets
hurrying to early shift-work. They turned toward the wharf. The
shortest of the women carried a baby in a sling across her back. The
child was swaddled to the chin and fast asleep. A brown bottle swung
from its mouth and the teat jerked flat with each short stride. All the
way to the ferry Humphrey walked to one side in case the bottle
dropped and splintered. He lost them in the crowd outside the
terminal.

And from his hotel room Humphrey booked for the breakfast
flight to Tokyo.

Our Famous Ladies

Humphrey expected someone would meet him at Haneda Airport.
He opened his bags on the customs counter and showed his
documents at the immigration stile, listening, but none of the
broadcast messages seemed to bear his name. He waited until the
crowds dispersed from his flight and took a taxi. The sky was overcast
and his breath frosted the side window though it was mid afternoon.
The journey seemed to take a long time. He could not tell if it was
the distance or the vituperative scrums of small, high-revving and

polished vehicles that choked into each intersection like a
homecoming of foraging insects.

He booked into the hotel and his bags disappeared with a bell-boy.
The receptionist handed him a message slip. He unfolded it. I look
forward to meeting you, he read, first round of talks tomorrow at
eleven. We should meet at this desk at nine. Be fit. It was signed:
Butcher, Mincorp. Humphrey screwed it up but could not throw it
away. He put it in his trouser pocket.

The hotel was immense and rose in twin cylinders so each room
gazed to a horizon. A jumbled grey spread as far as he could see. The
city reached so far that Humphrey could find no part with the scatty
and whimsical character of a periphery. Humphrey's floor was the
twenty-third. His window could not be opened and hissed in the
wind like an aircraft's porthole. The room was small and overheated
but he could find no thermostat so he lay on the cover of the bed in
his briefs and slept for four hours. When he woke, the room so
depressed him he left it without unpacking to walk the ancient and
fragrant gardens from which the buildings rose. As he stepped outside
he found the paths were unlit and it was raining.

He chose a European restaurant on the third level. Its Swiss cuisine
was impenetrable. He was used to following Mimi's lead when he ate
out, but he ordered a steak with a name he thought was pleasantly
frivolous and drank a bottle of Beaujolais while he waited. The steak
arrived marbled with fat. It's quite inedible, he said, fatty, though the
manager described the hours of peasants' fingers working its flavour
into the animal. Look, he told them, I don't care if you knew the
beast by name, and he ordered a salad.

Ground level was gay and busier than a railway station. Uniformed
girls directed traffic into elevators and stood outside as the doors
closed, white gloves clasped and heads bowed, as if its safe journey
was at the whim of their gods. Humphrey turned at a clatter of
applause and smiled at a group of tall young European men and
women, three abreast, a platoon, in blue blazers and white slacks.
Most were blond haired. They seemed identical in height and walked
with the bulky but resilient step of basketballers. The crowd parted to
let them through, but they looked directly ahead and parents pulled
their children out of the way.

Humphrey found a bar. He sat at a small corner table and ordered whisky and a split of soda. He drank only the whisky. The room was noisily lighthearted, though the crowd had the transient and inattentive air he remembered from shipboard farewells, an anticipation of events yet to come. He could see no girl drinking alone. He ordered another whisky. I need to find a girl, he asked the waiter, you understand? The waiter laughed. Sure, man, he said, I understand. He had the relaxed accent Humphrey associated with the American West Coast though he'd never been there. Just look around, there's girls all over, the waiter said, and walked away.

Humphrey wandered through the arcade toward the foyer. The boutiques were still trading though it must have been nearly midnight. Many of the windowshoppers were young Japanese women dressed in the styles of Paris and New York. Large picture hats were popular with women he guessed to be under thirty. He saw one girl walking alone and smiled at her but he was not noticed.

He walked through the foyer and onto the kerbed apron. There were three taxis. He slid into the front passenger seat of the first, can you take me to a girl, he asked. The driver did not answer him but bipped the horn twice, and Humphrey got out as the commissionaire in his uniform of an advancing general reached the front of the cab. Don't bother, Humphrey said, I've changed my mind.

In his room he flopped onto the bed without pulling the cover. He pulled off his tie and shoes. The room was as oppressive as a hot summer night. He stripped to his underpants and drank three glasses of water in the bathroom. He sat on the edge of the bed and sipped a whisky from the miniatures in the refrigerator.

He picked up the telephone as soon as he thought of it, I'll ring Mimi, but replaced the receiver before the trunks operator answered. Silly.

He lay on the bed and drew up a sheet against the breath of the airconditioner. He felt his skin drying out. It smelled like the curing of tobacco. He walked to the bathroom and showered, but the heat opened his pores so their oils laid the nap flat on the towel and he became stickier. He should have had a sauna, it may have sapped his manic restlessness. Perhaps it was not too late and he riffled the plastic pages of the hotel directory. Sauna, he found and dialled it, but the number did not answer.

It was not until he had poured another whisky that he thought of a massage. He looked again. Massage, it read, the most expert digital manipulation for your relaxing and good humour, our famous ladies will take all care, twenty-four hours. He rang and the call was quickly answered. Yes, we will send a girl to your room in a few minutes, please shower first.

Humphrey had soaped meticulously before he realised he had already showered. His towel was heavy with moisture. He was barely into white slacks and an open necked cheese-cloth shirt, Mimi had bought it for his birthday, when the doorbell rang.

She was very short. Humphrey could not place her age better than between fifty and seventy years. She propped in mid-room like a flag pony and swung around. You had shower? she asked. Humphrey nodded, his eyes had the moist honesty of a schoolboy's; two, he said.

Her quick tyranny had hurled him back thirty years. His aunt had had exactly this wash-house authority, words for cleanliness and godliness were often together in her mouth. The guardian of his motherless first year at high school, she interrogated his bedside prayers and was disgusted by the sight of bodily flesh so that the flapping of the open vent in his pyjama trousers was a nightmare his hand could never leave, what are you doing, and any truant thought of her holystone palms against his genitals whispered of misshapen and closeted children and tightened his stomach until his bowels ached. She smoothed the bedsheet. Humphrey stood in the corner and she handed him a towel. She had no smile for him.

She pointed to the bathroom and pushed him toward it. Her thrust made him stumble. Take all clothes off, she said. He stood in the bathroom doing nothing. She knocked on the door. Come out. He stripped off his clothes and wrapped the towel about his pimpling hips. He opened the door. There, she pointed to the bed. He lay with his hair lank on the pillow. She snatched the pillow away and his head dropped onto the sheet. She loosened the towel. Humphrey waited.

Now, she said. His tendons extruded like copper wires until she spoke again.

Now, she said, no funny business.

Between Whores

Humphrey ate breakfast in the hotel cafeteria. The menu was entirely western though most of the tables were occupied by Japanese. Apart from a muted clatter of metal and laminex the long room was quiet. There were almost no women. The men seemed to be of the category that marketers of unusually shaped swimming pools, lemon perfumed body chemicals or two-door coupes refer to as middle executive. They read precisely folded newspapers with irritable secrecy and blanched their coffee and apportioned their toast with an accuracy crucial in determining the humour of the growing day.

Humphrey caught movement from behind and turned.

Four young men walked to the table next to him. They were westerners and very tall. T-shirts stretched across their shoulders as tightly as over padding and each was stencilled with the shape of a football. Three of the men wore slacks. The legs of the fourth swung from black cotton shorts and thong sandals flopped under his feet. Dishevelled by recent sleep, they scraped into chairs with the heavy bumping of camping cattle. The odour of heavy bedclothes hung about them as tangibly as a cloud of flies.

Humphrey waited until they had finished eating and had ordered coffee. He leaned across, G'day, how's it going, he asked and he felt a sudden warmth in the accent as if the words had been unexpectedly spoken by someone else. They looked up almost together.

It was going OK, they said, but tired, what with three cities in eight days and that. They were, they told him, on a post-season holiday tour: Manila, Hong Kong, Tokyo, Honolulu, and now into their third Tokyo day. Six of the team had gone down with a dose of traveller's guts in Manila from eating the local food, wouldn't you know. It's OK here.

They were, perhaps, the four largest people Humphrey had ever spoken to in one group. During the season he followed the football but only by television. Though he scanned the Monday sports pages to memorise the commentators' phrases he used at coffee-breaks or in the staff rooms, he reacted to it all rather as if it were compulsory. Each of these four faces felt familiar to him but he recognised only one: a face with the deep grain of old leather and tendons knotting

the right side of his neck as though in a perpetual cramp. A half-back,
Humphrey remembered. Despite their size, each had a tentativeness
that surprised him. Perhaps it vanished when the team was together.
They gazed around the room but caught no one staring; there seemed
to be nothing familiar to grasp, so their fists lolled about on the
tabletop and sank into shapeless heaps like bags of children's marbles.

They were maliciously fit, Humphrey thought, at the cost of
thousands a head. Their club was sponsored, he knew something of it,
by the millionaire son of a coal-mining magnate who had broken the
transfer regulations by continuous and costly appeals to the Privy
Council. He had instituted training programmes to the regimen of a
military directorate and protected them with a lavish secretiveness
Humphrey suspected was designed only to propel the most
outrageous and impracticable rumour. Strides had been lengthened by
the finitesimal stretching of ligaments. The piston thrust of legs
compacted especially sprung footboards to increased girth. Hand grips
were strengthened by the ceaseless resilience of rubber orbs pumped
tight with stiff gases until their grasp could hold a football in the
span of an instant against any impact and they heaved the rasping
product of their lungs into exploding balloons the size of horses'
bellies set to levels predetermined by a physiology which could
communicate with them only in the metallic repetition of a fat
Bavarian whose moist fingertips tasted the sweat of human flesh
through the flickering orifice of a galvanometer; and the music of his
cassettes flowed into their soft headphones all the forgotten hatreds of
old tribes until their lips trembled with the justice of it and he slowly
turned down the rhythm of their cerebral responses on a meter the
size of an old-fashioned wireless set until its violet oscillations were
no longer discernible to the naked eye and they were, he smiled,
clinically dead. At this moment, he said, at this moment they are, he
said with his quickening tongue of a crazy metronome, at this
moment they are truly invincible.

    They lost the premiership on a play-off. Six days later a television
crew filmed the boarding of their flight to the Philippines. The team
posed with an immense toy kangaroo stitched from green and gold
velour. It took two of them to carry it. In a speech to the cameras,

their captain looked forward to the cultural centres of the orient. Evening editorials praised the use of sporting groups as ambassadors for their country. Their behaviour on the flight was boisterous. Twenty minutes short of Manila a stewardess discovered the kangaroo sitting on the toilet. Under the velour she found a sixteen-year-old cheer-squad leader who was wearing nothing else and was very drunkenly proud of being stuffed, as she kept saying, in a kangaroo over the territories of three nations. She was returned to Sydney on the next flight. The press described her as an ingenious and independent stowaway.

On the 28th of October the team was photographed in the white foyer of the Hotel Manila with the young soldier on duty who nervously watched the entrance as they posed with his American machine pistol and juggled three of his six grenades. On the 2nd of November they drove to a Hong Kong club and lunched in the pool despite the chill above its heated waters, floating beer cans to each other and playing water polo with a salad bowl carved from monkey-wood. In the afternoon they paused for three and a half minutes of silence during a broadcast of the Melbourne Cup though they would forget to observe two minutes' silence at eleven a.m. nine days later when thirteen million of their countrymen remembered the dead of two world wars, and most were reported to have later ascended Mount Victoria alongside Ernis Natoli (pictured), the flying forward and last year's Stawell Gift back-marker, who left them at the turnstiles and bounded two thousand one hundred steps to race the cable-car to the peak. Their evenings were never reported.

Humphrey asked if they had found the local talent, been out on the town, he said, jerking his head to one side as if he knew where it was. Sure they had, but he could feel no enthusiasm in them. Do any good, he asked?

Of course they had, but it was only his hint of assumed failure that drew a reply. They had been driven to the address of a cat bar, they called it, but could not remember seeing its name. They were expected, an arranged mixture of Japanese and European girls, the orders taken during a sight-seeing afternoon and transmitted by radio-telephone from the chartered bus en route to a cultural exhibition somewhere north of the city. A display of ancient cooking artifacts where they were to pose for P.R. photographs cabled back to the newspapers at home. They posed in rows of nine, three deep, in front of the huge hand-carved doors of the museum because the exhibition was closed.

They hesitated. Only the youngest player was eager to talk. He was an angular boy with long and muscular forearms, and, with his elbows on the table, had the posture of a mantis. Though he glanced at them, now and then, as if for correction, the others said nothing.

The bus trundled them south into a district that seemed familiar enough to be close to the hotel. It was nearly dark. They drank beer from cans taken from iceboxes stacked the length of the back bench and kicked the bloodied wrapping of hamburgers under the seats. Three of the younger players stood in the aisle and swung on handrails though there were many seats. Their singing had mostly tailed away. The seven older members of the club, Coach, the masseurs, officials, sat together in the front. The driver called through the PA: You, not throwing, he told them again, keep cans inside, against the law, he said. Coach leaned forward and patted his shoulder. It's OK, he said, it's OK.

Not until the bus slowed, blaring cars and taxi-cabs into the kerb, navigating impossible corners with its bulk of a rolling troop-barge and taking from gutter to gutter to do it – hey where're we going – were the narrow streets and thin shopfronts of timber shingles and postcard panes noticed at all. Round paper lamps in red and yellow and beads of party lights slid past them as close as a village on the bank of a canal. Coach took the PA. His hair bristled like a latrine brush and skin clung to his cheekbones as if it were wet from wading the warm lagoons of Sarawak and Fuok-Twi. He stood with his weight over his toes. Hear this, he said, no one is to disembark. This is a surprise.

The bus had stopped. Coach went inside a small building that could have been a delicatessen. Almost immediately he appeared again, and behind him women streamed from the doorway, in slack-suits, flowered kimonos, cocktail dresses, carrying handbags, satchels, overnight cases, in singles and pairs and threes toward the bus. The Coach pressed them into single file with one arm stiff as a semaphore.

With the other he appeared to be counting by twos.

The first woman lifted the hem of her kimono high enough to step up into the bus. Though no older than twenty-two she seemed to be having difficulty. On the top step she began smiling and her lacquered hair shone with its three hours of preparation. Her gaze was on the floor. In silence she bowed to the driver and turned to face them all: the twenty-one athletes again greasy with sweat, and the trainers whose chunky fingers still smelled of bruised eucalyptus leaves and secret oils wrung from the bellies of strangled mutton birds, and the three officials too tired to stand. Perhaps she was awaiting welcome.

Only one of them spoke. Well, he said, and it was the youngest player in his spiralling voice of a club-room jester, well, I said, somebody opened a packet of whores.

The sudden winds of their laughter bit into her face and she turned a little as though slightly off balance. When she straightened, her smile was wide but a wisp of hair had fallen over her forehead and her eyes looked swiftly from side to side for nothing they could understand. The Coach leaned inside and pushed her from behind. It's OK, he said, it's OK.

The twenty-eight women were smuggled into the hotel through the basement entrance. They hid giggles behind hands softened with lotion or held the hands of others or pressed clasped hands to their small bosoms in the humble attitudes westerners associate only with prayer and bowed quietly to the Bell Captain who had agreed to arrange their prohibited journey. He drafted them into four groups without fuss and into the goods lifts.

On the eighteenth floor the Coach paired girls and players – hey who's going to play on me – and repeatedly calling for silence allocated in the order of their club numbers. I'm choosing the best I can by size, he said – the size of what, they yelled – until with the holding of waists and the twining of fingers a promenade along the darkened corridors had already begun, and the Coach held up his hand again for silence. He took the elbow of an elderly man, dressed in white slacks and the piped blazer of a club official, and shuffled him between two girls. The girls were unsmiling and wore plain red kimonos. The old man had the unhappy and defenceless grin of one who fears a practical joke. He was the club's Most Ardent Supporter. Tonight, the Coach said to him with the cellophane smile of a television compere, is to be the night of your life.

The club's Most Ardent Supporter had thirty years' unbroken attendance at fund-raising dinners. The previous record was twenty-five. A fit and reserved man, he celebrated his agelessness by running with the team on Friday jogs, his brown pate glistening with a breathless dew. He swam in the sea every morning and evening of his adult life, summer and winter, and shaved the daily grey stubble from his temples so that his head shone in the sunshine. He was treated as the club mascot, and allowed to carry the club standard onto the ground at important games. At the twenty-sixth dinner they noticed something was awry. He drank alcohol, though he was a teetotaller, an abstinence he treasured before retiring as a provincial bank manager. At each dinner his behaviour became worse, and at the last he made childish and shameful gestures, angered the waitresses and fell backwards from his chair. Within a month he was retired as mascot, amid a profusion of gratitude from thankful officials and despite his confused protests that he would maintain an active loyalty until the day he died. He was made an award. A token, through roars of applause and laughter, of their appreciation: to be despatched with the players on the annual tour. He was only able to mumble his thanks, before early applause drowned him out.

In his hotel room, the Most Ardent Supporter was stripped of his clothes. I can do it myself, he said, but Coach and two of the players pushed him into the shower and made him scrub under needles of hot water that billowed with steam and his anger that it might weaken his strength for the rigours to come. It did not. His loins flexed with anticipation. The two women waited silently in the corridor. In the bathroom he hurriedly shaved. Mopping his cheek with stained tissue and wrapped in a bathrobe, he was lifted into the bedroom and slid under a white sheet as crisp as any hospital bed. Propped against three pillows, he flexed his arm muscles in a gesture of virility. The door was opened. Visiting time.

The Coach led the women into the bedroom. He loudly hummed the tune he knew as Big Spender. One of the women placed a plastic case on the table and opened it with a click. In it they saw grey cotton bags, openings glinting with the ends of chromed metal, and a canvas bundle round with things soft and pliable. She took out two strong rubber bands and snapped them onto her fingers.

We are taking about two, she looked under the sheet, about four hours. Part of the sheet had folded into a small tent. The Most Ardent Supporter raised one knee to hide it.

They lasted, the boy said looking at Humphrey, about three. Everyone else got laid in their rooms, he said. Some of the girls had gone and it was quiet. Then I began to hear this wail.

Through the walls, under the door, around the window-sills, a thin sound, without hope of relief, a cry existing simply for its own sound. No one wanted to answer. But on and on it ran in a continuous line of anguish. They found her in the corridor, on one knee, head down as though searching for something in the deep carpet. They lifted her up. Her hand covered the left side of her neck. She looked wide into their faces, and floated her hand away. On the side of her pale neck were the red prints of the crimped grasp she had had to prise away.

Humphrey grabbed for more coffee. The roaring old stud, he said, swollen with rubber thongs and slippery with lotion, out of control and onto her?

No. The half-back spoke to him for the first time.

We fly him out this afternoon. He died.

Humphrey sat at the table for more than a full minute. The silence was his only path back to propriety. For the last few seconds it was the quietness of a small house painted the garish black and green of club colours, of trophy cups rigidly shoulder to shoulder the length of a still mantelpiece, of the inconsolable drawing of blinds.

Humphrey drained his coffee and stood up. Well, he said, take care.

Dreaming of Glory

The restaurant was once a golf-house. Trophy cases in the hallway still displayed the chromium shapes of putting irons and golf balls and a wood that was once the instrument of a hole-in-one by a member of the Imperial Family. The names of winners of Japanese tournaments were celebrated on rosewood panels high on the wall. The titles were all in English. Old photographs of uncomfortable golfers in plus-fours and cloth caps were mounted on both sides of the doorway. Humphrey had not seen them when he came in. He was surprised to find a date as early as 1919.

He found Butcher and the four Japanese delegates already on the terrace. They were not waiting for him. Butcher struggled into the flaccid burden of his overcoat and his gasps fumed into the cold afternoon as if he were puffing at a cigar. He turned his back for Humphrey to lift the coat by its collar and held out his arms in the half-mast gesture of a heavy knight readied for the fray. Higher, he grunted, higher.

Their limousines had waited through lunch under trees at the edge of a driveway that touched the building only for a moment before curling back to the road. The guard box had a despondent air as if it were empty. The chauffeurs opened the car doors wide. Three hours of slow rain had speckled the gun-metal panels with the sunset red and amber of autumn maples and the windows had fogged with condensation from motors running to keep the drivers warm. Butcher wrapped the flaps of his overcoat about his thighs and took the last space in the rear of the first car. He took time to settle himself. Humphrey stooped to climb into the front. No, Butcher called to him, you ride with the others. He waved to the driver to close the doors and Humphrey turned away.

Humphrey rode in the front of the second car. Though conversation at lunch had been brisk, and often jolly, the two Japanese sitting behind him fell silent and only occasionally pointed out places that might be of interest to a foreigner. The traffic into Tokyo was heavy and slow in the wet. They crossed the river Sumida by a stone bridge Humphrey was told was famous for its age, and swung into the river-side boulevard. The kerb was lined with riot police.

For nearly two kilometres they picketed the sidewalk at intervals Humphrey judged to be ten paces. Every plane and articulation of their bodies was cased in black cladding and the carapaces gleamed with the intensity of wet paint although the light was dull. Their scaled fists held staves upright in unwavering enfilades for as far as

Humphrey could see. There must be hundreds. Narrow shields hung from their forearms with no emblazonment of heraldry so that they seemed to be responsible to no identifiable authority. Each visor reflected an unyielding and malevolent glaze behind which Humphrey could find no flicker of life and sloped at an angle that recalled nothing so much as an iron mandible.

The cars turned off the boulevard at a roadblock that had not been there before lunch and Humphrey felt a relief he thought was very foolish. He turned to Hogara. Why, he asked, were there so many police?

Hogara shrugged. Today, I don't know, he said. Maybe the safe movement of some important people, he smiled, big shots.

The air of the conference room was still stale from the morning session. Its warmth was welcome. Humphrey sat on the same side of the long table as Butcher but left an empty chair between them. He expected to take no part in this final and summary session. He had taken no part in the earlier three. On the morning of the first meeting Butcher had tapped with his thick finger the brief and its twenty-eight appendices; he asked Humphrey if he was familiar with the figures. I am the author, Humphrey told him with a smile, of their every digit; if you have any trouble, just ask. I see, Butcher had said, your reward for diligence, I wondered why you were here. I will do the talking, he said, I'm going to pitch it to them.

Butcher began. His voice had the stock-in-trade confidence of a door-to-door salesman. He had, Humphrey knew something of it, joined Mincorp as a publicist for petroleum extracts after a year with Lancia in Turin, he had spent two years as advertising manager for one of the toolmakers of the Ruhr and had directed promotion for a breakfast cereal, a brand of low-tar cigarettes and an expanding line of executive games from California. He had less German and Italian than he claimed. I am a marketing man, he said, as if there were no higher credential.

Humphrey thought of Butcher as having the mannered bonhomie of an anglican prelate. It seemed unmanly and unvirtuous to disagree with anything he said. His weight must have been over a hundred kilos but at parties he danced intricately and with a sureness in his own centre of gravity that unnerved his partners and they clung petulantly to him. His headstrong driving had killed his first wife and Humphrey had met only his second, a singer he had married in Munich. He spoke as though misfortune had deprived her of leading roles in Marschner and Wagner but sometimes late at those parties her voice made the vulnerable and searching notes of the blues and her thighs worked the slits in her skirt. She was not often with him. If asked about it, Butcher told of their asthmatic daughter whose sickness stifled her frantic breath at unpredictable, he said, and inconvenient hours.

None of the four Japanese took notes while Butcher spoke. Their blue folders lay on the table. All were executives of the same company, a corporation of immense size and diversification, through the baking of plastics, the harvesting of foodstuffs and the invention of pesticides. And all were from the plastics division; the plastic arm of your corporate body, Humphrey had said as they first met, but everyone seemed to be smiling already, and one after the other exchanged business cards with him, accepting Humphrey's always with the left hand then holding the card toward him at arm's length in the expectation of a motionless instant, beginning with the minute narrowing of an eye's aperture and ending in the sudden flash of a smile, so that card and face were together printed in a single frame of permanent cognition. They bowed him on with a grateful excitement which Humphrey found impossible not to parody a little in return.

Strangely, Butcher had become uncomfortable and sat behind his placecard at the table before he realised the introductions were incomplete. Perhaps he was nervous. I want you to show complete attention, he had whispered to Humphrey, do you realise how important this deal is to us? Yes, Humphrey said, I do indeed.

Humphrey opened his folder, slowly so as not to distract them and turned the pages of 'What's On In Tokyo'. He passed quickly over advertisements for orchestral concerts, Japanese traditional theatre and movies. Massage parlours, skin flicks, escort agencies and night clubs took up the last four pages. He marked 'Charon, intimate, drinks from 600 yen small beer, English speaking hostesses, piano music with song'. And on the last line: 'stress'. Oh, songstress.

He drew out another pamphlet. It had the rectangular shape of a travel guide but its pages were firm and glossy with a bulky presence. It was a public relations brochure for the Japanese corporation he had plucked from a display box in the foyer.

Although the text stood in inaccessible lines of characters with the teetering columnar quality of alphabet blocks, the pictures were captioned also in English. A frontispiece laid together a montage of ships at dock, against paddy fields and office blocks and textile looms, all to promote the variety of the corporation's enterprise. Although Humphrey had researched these painstakingly for his masters, he had found and dealt out merely figures, quantifications and categories. Here the incidences of effort were displayed as if through an opening of windows in the page: these looms hummed with countless threads unravelling the warp and weft of the spectrum; mimicking rows of rice plants wore a fresh and humid green from the flush of morning rains; painters in bosuns' chairs swung against the iron side of a ship and painted over spreading ink stains that had wept from her blundering deck on bitter southern nights as deck-bins overflowed the slime of squid dying in their thousands under a cold halogen glare visible for as many miles as the far corona of a small city.

A chart gave the corporation's income over a decade. Its yearly turnover ranked twelfth of the companies of the world and was exceeded by the revenue of only fourteen national governments. A photograph showed three chartkeepers marking a map of countries bordering the Pacific Ocean with points of their company's conquest. Their mouths were bunched from sucking rows of sharp pins like ageing seamstresses. Humphrey looked up. That chart hung on the wall opposite him. The seaboards glittered with coloured pin-heads but its surface was surprisingly faded and the clusters did not match those in the photograph.

On another page the executives of Plastics Division sat, as they did at this meeting, behind nameplates in the manner of a press conference. Okura, Inter-Group Liaison, speaks English with a Cambridge accent; the tiny Production Co-ordinator Hogara acts also as an interpreter for Kogo of Finance, who will try no English at all and scratches marks into his agenda margin but does not take them with him overnight; Shimizu, Marketing, brown from much golf at his club where green fees of each game cost more, he will tell you, than a labourer's monthly wage, and chatters only about sport over lunch in his high tone of an excited spectator; and other faces from other divisions and other places, all photographed in the foreground of factories so their capacity for industry is incontrovertible, or before attentive groups of scribbling trainees, or behind busy desks and holding a calculator or a pen warily still only for the interruption of the snapshot. None of them had the appearance of being, even momentarily, at rest.

Butcher paused at Hogara's politely diffident port de bras and coffee was served at a buffet table at the end of the room. The lacquered cups were of paper lightness and painted with a small and modular emblem reminding Humphrey of a pagoda: the mark of the company president, Hogara told him as he faced Humphrey toward a portrait on the wall, holding him by the elbow with a flattering courtesy as if introducing him to an ancestor. The portrait was of an old man, perhaps in his seventies, and of a sepia quality that may have been either of emulsion or of pigment. The figure sat in an elaborately carved and high-backed chair. Yes, Humphrey said, I noticed it earlier.

Butcher began to close his summary, the run home, he put it. He used the shiny phrases of car yards and appliance show-rooms directed across the polished table to Shimizu. Shimizu is the opinion-maker of this group, Butcher had said after the first session in his didactic voice of a business journal, every grouping has one. Shimizu is the power-broker.

Their case finished. Butcher asked for questions, for clarification, he put it, of our proposition. But it was the tiny Hogara who asked them while the others were silent, and who recorded with the quick strokes of a court reporter and with an interest only in the fulsomeness of the answers, as if their worth was a matter for some absent tribunal.

Humphrey found Hogara's president on the last page of the brochure. There were two pictures of him. In the first, he sat in a miniature of the sepia portrait on the wall. Underneath him were nine pillars of Japanese text and a photograph with the harsh shadows of a newspaper reproduction: a prayer offering, Humphrey thought at first, on the deck of a ship; a red-necked and awkward solemnity at a blessing of the fleet. But the faces have none of the compressed anticipation of waiting fishermen. Their posture is strict and their eyes are not on the sea but on the sky. They are airmen.

The president Shikoru is small for the chair carved with four hundred and seventy years of tumbling chrysanthemum petals but sits precisely in the centre of them with a frail dignity, on the light bones of the carefully aged, his spectacled eyes the fading grey of incense drifting in the wake of solemn processions, his white shirt-collar stiffly hiding folds in his throat with the mute decorum of a Shinto cassock. He sits easily still. The grey pin-striped suit is exactly pressed. Slim hands lie gently folded in his lap. His fingers wear no ring.

Every morning he rises a half hour before dawn and, wrapped in the plain kimono of the bereaved, walks from his bare sleeping-room across a marbled courtyard. His wooden sandals make always four slow beats over the narrow timbers of the bridge, above the ancient carp whose silken tails lazed, as his son had said in childhood, to hold their sleeping in mid-stream; through a low doorway and into the consecrated cell to wait before its stone shrine, his wisping head bowed during the perceptible bleaching of walls, until first light darkens the frame of a photograph fastened above the altar and he can again begin to make out the raised eyes of the boy-pilot and his ghosted reflection in the curved cowling of a fighter plane already trembling with the deafening heat of the last long thunder. Twenty-eight tilted wings in a herringbone pattern across the flight deck in hard crosses behind one and a half rows of tomorrow's faces, fourteen, again he counts them, rigidly to attention; and standing alone facing the boy is the braided figure of a Flag Officer of the Imperial Forces, his rimless spectacles misting in the salt air, the silver imprimatur of the Emperor's own command heavy on his shoulders. His steady fingers hold a white scarf to the boy's neck, the banner of sacrifice fluttering in the photograph's instant. The Commander's thin throat is already too old for his prime, his hair is wisping and his eyes fade in the grey wake of five years' war.

When he can no longer see the detail of that day beyond his misting spectacles he leans forward and again kisses the chill over his son's glazed face and again draws back only far enough to whisper to him the soft syllables: Heiwa.

Peace.

Re-crossing the narrow bridge he feeds the carp.

Some illusions can assume the status of truth. Humphrey knew it no longer mattered that the details of his day-dreaming were invented and hallucinatory. He knew, in a way now indelible and complete, that this Japanese corporation is guided, not with the careful powers of delegation drawn from the teachings of London or Harvard, but in the manner of a kingdom, of old and familic loyalties and enmities, for which the tabular logic of immediate opportunity and risk are of incidental interest. Decisions will be taken only by this ageing ruler or those related to him through a lineology of belief in the nobility of ultimate conquest and the knowledge that time is not measured merely in terms of the accountant's year, or the historian's war.

Humphrey was suddenly aware he was the centre of an expectant silence. He closed the folder. I'm sorry, he said, I didn't catch that. He looked along the table. They looked at him with the counterfeit enthusiasm of their subordinate authorities. None of them ranked as – he thought of Hogara's use of the words – big shots. I said, Butcher repeated while the others waited, that about wraps it up. Yes, Humphrey said, I'm sure it does.

On the stairs Butcher slowed him by the sleeve so they lagged behind. We are going great, Butcher said, Shimizu asked us for drinks and dinner. I said you fly out early in the morning; I want him alone, okay? He did not wait for a reply. On the ground floor his stride was long and his arms swung. Humphrey trailed to the position of an adjutant. Sure, Humphrey said, pitch it to him.

A Sense of Propriety

I

Humphrey's wife is a modest person. To her friends, Mimi is an arbiter of taste whose values are as authoritative as the deft eye of an arts critic. Her judgements have a rightness about them, they tell her, an instinctive sagacity, though she does not yet admit to being forty-five. She is clearheaded. As an executive member of an anti-vivisection group, proofs of the need to legislate death penalties for murder, rape and incest also come easily to her. Mimi admits the vigour and industry of people successful in commerce, but speaks of Humphrey's capacity for diligence only in a sorrowful tone. Showiness repels her, yet an enjoyment of those small displays that position and income allow, she will tell you without embarrassment, has never left her.

She now entertains only at restaurants, but for many years Mimi held a dinner-party at home every three or four weeks. Her preparations were always the same. She extended the dining table by four panels, unlocked the crystal cabinet with a key she kept hidden in her wardrobe, and bought a new pair of shoes. From an agency she hired a woman to work as a scullery maid for the preparation of the food and to later wait, in pinafore and lace cap, at table during dinner. In the afternoon they chilled oysters in half shell, dusted a Chateaubriand with powders of a herb mixture Mimi said had been her gossipy grandmother's only secret, and folded together the stiffening ingredients of an orange mousse. Mimi selected a platter of cheeses and arranged them so no two of a similar style or similar region lay together. She believed this heightened the noises of discovery. There is nothing worse, she said, than a dull party.

She allowed one deviation. Sometimes, in winter, the mousse was chocolate. Humphrey remembered one crown roast of lamb, but its cage of thin bones, Mimi thought, suggested a starvation inconsistent with hearty provender and she never served it again.

Humphrey watched these preparations with a growing gloom. They promised a divertissement of manners for which their home was no fit theatre. The house was proud but had difficulty presenting a justification for its pride. It held neither the mystery of a barely understood age nor the excitement of experiment in texture and symmetry. Its extended en suite bedrooms, library and poolside bungalow might have grown to the commands of a merchant whose fortunes were never predictable. And Humphrey could not welcome their guests with the outstretched and elaborate charm Mimi expected of him. Increasingly he was unavoidably late on these evenings and sometimes he arrived closely after the first couples.

There were seldom new faces. The guests did not need to be told where to sit. Three of the ladies were friends from Mimi's university days: Doris, married to a solicitor who corrected what he said were faults in her argument; Bella and her Wolf imported European wines and sold them on mail order through their cellar club; Catherine's Francis grew beef in central Queensland by a remote control Humphrey could never understand. And always, there were the Fitzherberts.

The Fitzherberts were late. Max Fitzherbert telephoned at eight to apologise for Edwina's illness, it had hounded her now for some days, and he was particularly sorry, Edwina is too, he said, we guessed the reason for this gathering: Mimi's wedding anniversary two days earlier. Mimi was quickly upset. Edwina is one of my best, my very best friends in all the world, she said, but she persuaded Max to join them for coffee and liqueurs.

The agency had sent a Rumanian maid who sometimes forgot to address Mimi as Madam, and carried the imperious bearing of unforgotten nobility which they joked about when she was out of the room and tittered about when she was not. Kate at last admired Mimi's shoes, it was the only contribution to the conversation she had made all night, giving Mimi her opportunity to say she chose them only for comfort, although the heels were four inches long and Humphrey knew they gave her an aggregate height of six feet and an inch. Finally, two independent remarks were made about the cheese, Mimi relaxed, and the guests began to leave.

Still flushed from the port, Humphrey thought the last guests had gone. He showered, leaving Mimi's towel ready for her over the end of the marbled bath. She might be still clearing away. He wrapped his own towel about him and walked into the passageway. He stopped at the door of the diningroom as Mimi closed its French windows. Max Fitzherbert was leaving the patio. The glass panels rippled as he moved. Where have you been? Humphrey asked her. Mimi started. She had not heard him enter. Saying goodbye to Max, she said, his

141

company is moving him to Sydney. I wonder why he didn't mention it, Humphrey said, I should phone him.

Eight weeks later, Mimi held her next party. The Fitzherberts' place was filled by Nancy and Jack Sullivan. Nancy had wandered the periphery of Mimi's friendship for some years but had not progressed. Her father had owned a scrap-metal lot of undetermined size, within a mile of the city centre, until he was killed in 1942. Her mother took it over. She refused to employ anyone but two Alsatian dogs and boasted that she knew the exact location of every fractured stainless sink, wire hawser, green copper boiler, hoop of metric washers, left-side Ford fender, and rusty bugle in the precarious and impossible jumble of that yard. Perhaps she did. Her son became a priest and she sent each of her four daughters to private schools for young ladies. She slept and cooked in the shed she used for an office, wore whiskered slippers and an army great-coat, and her heaving breath smelled of methyl spirit. Her daughters wrote to her less and less. When she died – last spring, Humphrey had read of it, after the viciously cold winter – newspapers referred to her simply as Old Maggie, as their columnists had sporadically for thirty years. Her estate was later valued for Probate at five million dollars. The twelve confectionery jars of old coins were worth an ordinary fortune. Within a few months the daughters began to come out. They were photographed picnicking at the races and the gowns they wore to charity balls were described in the women's weeklies. Not all of this was due to the meticulous conduits of heritage, for some was diverted. Much was claimed by a wide-eyed and affronted Taxation Department who had never heard of her and quickly sought a court declaration of the present value of fifty thousand pounds in mildewed bank-notes. Most was given, devised and bequeathed to the Catholic Church in this the last Will and Testament of me Margaret Mary O'Dowd being of sound mind and full testamentary capacity written in painstaking longhand between the paragraphs of a form of Will that cost her two shillings and sixpence at Wilkenson & Burridge Law Stationers and was not much younger than any of the lawyers who were asked if they could break it. No, Humphrey knew, money was not the agency that eased Nancy Sullivan's homecoming to the peers of her childhood. She was released by the page two heading of an evening newspaper. Old Maggie Dies.

By nine-thirty Jack and Nancy Sullivan had so smoothly fitted into the façade of the group it was difficult, Humphrey thought, to see the joins. They admired the Chateaubriand and were captivated by the cheese. Their frequent and off-handed use of the christian names of friends common to them all established their tartan and they were careful to refer by surname only to an outlander. It appeared that nothing had changed. Only Mimi seemed slightly off-touch.

The Sullivans spoke about the Fitzherberts first.

Humphrey wondered why someone had not mentioned them before. Nancy knew Edwina Fitzherbert loved Sydney. She had said in her letter that it was the beginning of a new life. Such a cliché, but you can understand, Nancy said in her frank voice of a New England finishing school. But Max. Nancy could not imagine. He had put Safpak on the map in the southern States, she felt sorry for him.

No, Sweet, Jack said while the rest of them were silent, No, he said, Max asked for his transfer.

Someone, perhaps Kate, as Humphrey later remembered it, swung the conversation in another direction. Mimi stood up from the table. Humphrey saw that her face was wan and her eyes were empty. She left to check the kitchen for more coffee, she said.

Before they went to bed, Mimi caught him in her dressing-table mirror. He was watching her from the doorway. Her voice was sharp: What are you staring at? A cleansing pad extinguished the tints and lights of her face like the dimming of a paper lampshade. I'm sorry, he said, that you have lost Edwina. She was a good friend.

Yes, Mimi said. Thanks.

The following week Humphrey was sent to Perth by his company. He was there two days. He knew no one well and after dinner he sat in front of the television in his motel-room and drank whisky until he fell asleep. Company travellers often suffer sadly after evenings spent that way, but Humphrey slept deeply, awoke hungrily to the tapping on his door of a cheerful and honest breakfast, showered, and stepped briskly into the day. He had seldom felt so fit. Perhaps it was because winter was suspended by his change of latitude. He found that the angular girl at the reception desk had a deceptive and thoughtful charm he had previously mistaken for surliness, and the number of

143

girls shopping the crowded streets, in skirts the bright colours of an early summer, had increased since he arrived. It occurred to him that he and Mimi should take a holiday.

From the return flight he took a cab directly to his office. The building was dark and everyone had gone for the night. Humphrey dropped a handwritten report into his secretary's typing tray and left a note she would find on her typewriter carriage on Monday morning telling her to cancel the week's appointments and that he would ring her that afternoon from wherever he was.

He went home.

When he opened the front gate he found four newspapers in the letterbox. He stepped over two cartons of milk on the front steps. The silence of the house was broken only by the turning of his key. He walked through all the rooms, not because Mimi might be somewhere there, but to wake them with his own movement, to lift the chill of emptiness from them. The rooms seemed unnaturally large, of course it is merely the stillness, but he could not shake off the feeling that he was frailer than he remembered himself, that he was somehow diminished.

And is any space as timeless as a deserted house? The grandfather clock in the corridor tapped at the wall to the walking-stick strokes of a blind old man, but in that corridor there was no time. In the dining-room, the brass orbs of a French mantelpiece clock twirled with the grace of a silent minuet, as they had, by the judgement of their own intervals, for a hundred and fifty years, but in the dining-room there was no time. A clock on the kitchen wall beat to the passage of parading electrons, not to commands from the march of time. Their clicking parody of time was a pitiless chronology of missed opportunity and loss. Remember the time?

Humphrey left all the lights in the hall, bedrooms, kitchen and dining-room burning. He poured a whisky and drank it in the kitchen. It was the brightest room in the house. The warmth of the whisky reminded him that his body was cold and he went to the dressing-room for a cardigan. Mimi's dressing-room table was bare. He flung open her wardrobe. She had taken very little, as far as he could tell, and her suits and dresses and gowns moved through his gaze in a pageant of happier times. Shoes littered the closet floor and were suddenly as dear to him as the foibles of a gifted and p sionate child. Why has she gone?

Humphrey ran to the ringing of the telephone with a shameless and awkward haste he would not have used if he were not alone. He wondered how long it had been ringing. He stifled his breathlessness. It was Mimi, he knew it before she spoke, he heard her gather her breath for the assault.

Where have you been? she shouted.

So Humphrey drove to join her at the coast.

The journey generally took an hour and a half. He had not been able to decide whether her annoyance was genuine. Perhaps he had told her that he would be back about midday. Perhaps, as she said, she had expected to telephone him at the office and tell him where she was. He had no difficulty remembering the way, even without Mimi to prompt him. He entered the township and took the coast road. The hotel had bungalows that opened onto the beach. He had taken Mimi there for the second night of their honeymoon, and four or five times since. The last with the Fitzherberts. Perhaps they should invite the Sullivans.

Humphrey knocked on the door of her bungalow a few minutes before midnight. He had to knock twice. The wind off the sea was cold but it had stopped raining.

As Mimi opened the door he saw she was drunk. She held a drink in one hand and held onto the door with the other. She wore a transparent negligee gathered at the throat with a black ribbon and her body was misty as if he could not quite focus on it. He did not know she owned clothes like that.

She held open the door. Come in, she said. Her smile was slightly late as though the sound she heard of her voice and the picture she had of her smile were not precisely synchronised. Come in, Honey, and she waved him inside with a sweep of her glass. She kicked the door closed behind him. Her feet were bare and the thrust of her kick was reckless and pagan. Draining the glass, she threw it onto the sofa. Her arms climbed around his neck. Without her shoes she was nearly his height.

I have waited a long time for something like this to happen, she told him, and threw back her head, apparently remembering how

145

long. Humphrey could give no reply but: I'm sorry, I drove as fast as I could.

Mimi fingered the lapel of his jacket as though insultingly assessing his worth. I have decided, she said, it might be time to take you as my lover. She held out the end of her black ribbon. Her voice was breathy. It seemed to be drawn from a moist place low in her belly. Humphrey had never heard that voice before.

Now, she said, undo me.

Humphrey took her ribbon in his fingers. He was bewildered by the discovery of Mimi's skill as a vamp but the astonishing lustfulness of it seduced him quickly. Her lascivious capture of him with the impudence of a slut gave him a heady buoyancy and lifted him over the impediments to manliness he found at lower psychological altitudes; she had thrown into the wind the modesties and proprieties with which she had been born to save their marriage from the farting and egg-bound boredoms of middle age, and he was suddenly proud to be spouse to such a peremptory and imaginative woman, and contemptuous of adulterers hiding behind derisive entries in motel registers and fogging wind-screens of darkly parked automobiles, he was cuckolding them all; I will take her in a way she has never known, and the expanding mass of his phallus would become the implement of his mastery and he began to pull on the ribbon, yes, he said, but his fingers jerked as if with an epilepsy of their own, yes, he said, it is time.

Don't be so nervous, she said, and her voice was already a sneer and the sound of it washed him down so that the sweat in his shirt clung to his chest with the sudden chill of wet cloth. Don't be so nervous, she said, you couldn't do worse than my husband.

The deep whooping of her laughter turned to coughing. She was pale and unsteady. Humphrey thought she was going to be ill but she was already asleep as he laid her on the bed. She looked so sick. He must stay beside her but he lay so their bodies did not touch. The night was already interminable.

Humphrey woke to find his wife had gone. She must have begun the drive back to the city soon after first light. He was surprised that she left him no note.

II

Only on Humphrey's last night in Tokyo did he find a whore.

Humphrey first saw her pushing towards him between the girls surrounding him at the bar. She was a European. He had been inside that bar for less than four minutes and was already very nervous. He could not answer all their greetings. Some were in Japanese. Others he should have been able to understand. He had not expected to be their only customer. The bar appeared so alive from the street. He had quickly ordered a whisky. When this girl spoke to him in English, Humphrey smiled at her with relief, as though she were merely unexpectedly late for their appointment.

She was an American, and with the thin bones and light skin that American films associate with estates in Maine and Massachusetts. She was blond, but with shorter hair than Mimi, and wore the longest boots he had ever seen. They were a shiny black, and reached so closely to the middle of her thighs that barely a hand's breadth separated them from the tail of her black leather jacket. The illusion of a carnal interval was astonishing, but a second glance saw jersey tights the bare-back colour of a palomino pony. Pulled rakishly over her forehead she wore a black cloth cap the peaked shape used by Irish poachers and British motor-cyclists in the twenties. The boots looked so stiff that Humphrey was surprised she could bend at the knee.

Sure, she knew his hotel. She handed him a card. I go there often, she said, any time you ring I'll be there. Humphrey let her count out from the lump of notes he took from his pocket. Thirty thousand fee and five for the drinks. She flipped it across the bar, using the end of her cigarette case as a croupier's trowel. She spoke to the barman. He nodded. We can go now, she said.

She led the way. Humphrey followed her between tables where girls from paddy-field families in central Honshu and from lane-side kiosks in Bangkok and from the dry back blocks of Houston played cards in fours and sixes, read old magazines; past the gaze of a coughing red-head in green culottes who had earlier turned away when Humphrey said no, I have no taste for gays, and no sooner was he gone than this American was in his place, what you see is what you get with me, Honey, she smiled, and, as he held her card tightly in his hand, she dealt out his money with the quick fingers of the gambling world; he followed her past the red pay-phones bolted to a peg-board bench over which rows of stapled note paper and short pencils hung on knotted string, and he stepped suddenly out onto the sullen footpath as cigarette smoke from the open doorway rolled under a pale streetlamp, as fine as winter mist.

Humphrey helped her on with her top-coat. It was heavy, with a tight nap, and reminiscent of a pedigreed black retriever Mimi had before they were married. It was difficult also because the girl was tall. But Humphrey had learned to be comfortable with tall women. Early in their marriage – what, twenty-one, twenty-two years ago? – he had thought of Mimi's height as a facet of her grace which reflected well on him. Sly glances of admiration, and whispered conversations he suspected were about her, all made him smile happily. Now, Mimi had developed a habit at parties of standing close to him so she could speak easily over his head.

My name is Anita, the girl told him, but she could not make it sound like any name mentioned for her at her christening. As they walked to the corner, and Humphrey wondered if he should have taken her hand, she established that it was his last night in Tokyo, that he had been here four days, and had seen little of the night-life. Can I show you the town? She asked. Humphrey nodded. Sure, he said with a slow-motion swankiness he would never have tried on Mimi, the night is still young. He looked at his watch. It was then barely midnight.

She hailed a cab. Humphrey opened the door and stood back for her to enter. My, she said, an unusual courtesy in this country. Her voice was without ridicule. He had made the sort of mistake his wife would have laughed at but his young whore had not. He felt instantly gallant and held her elbow as she climbed inside.

Later, Humphrey's memory would be unable to distinguish between any of the three bars they visited. Each was at ground level, they entered from identically narrow and crowded streets, more than half of their tables were unoccupied, and a crooning pianist included a round of Moon River in his repertoire. At the third, Humphrey asked her if Moon River was a Japanese Astronaut's Cirrhosis, but her smile was pale and she replied that she had not heard it so, and he turned instead to questions about her childhood in America. She seemed willing enough to tell him about it, and showed him photographs of her family that disturbed him strangely, and he broke it off. The waitresses who tended them thanked Anita rather than Humphrey for the generous tips she encouraged him to give. As they left, he found the light barely bright enough to read the exorbitant amount written on his check. He realised he had lost the sharp prodding of his lustfulness in the whirlwind conquest, as he now thought of it, of this stylish and vivacious courtesan, but it should return.

On the way to a casino, they turned past the Club Asakasa where, the night before, Humphrey had bought a strip of tickets to hold the devotion of a plump woman from the steep and misted mountain-slopes of Tajima, she told him, dressed in black organza to the ankle, who twitched her bosom often as though it were itching. Unexpectedly during their silences, she laughed with a secret merriment Humphrey slowly gathered was flirtatious. She poked at his chest and nudged his knee with a salacious jollity he found increasingly evocative, a grossness consistent with lust he had forgotten since the dormitory and toilet-block days of his high school. She might talk dirty and pour a drink into his mouth while it spilled from his lips with their laughter. She might squeeze his appetite for her into an obesity. He excused himself briefly to go to the toilet. At the urinal he had difficulty maintaining his flow, and when it finished, he did not feel the satisfaction of emptiness. He supposed it had to do with the irritable compulsiveness in his organ. It took him some time to arrange his uncomfortable genitals. When he walked back to the table his mountain woman had gone. Humphrey paid his bill at the cashier's box. He saw the woman at a table by the door. She had joined a noisy party of fifteen. He watched her twitching her bosom.

The casino was illegal, she told him, laughing at his nervousness, but it was safe. It lay in part of the basement of an office building. A darkened ground floor above them was taken up by the rich silence of a bank. The blank door to the gambling house swung open before Anita had pressed the buzzer. The doorman was an immense and flagrant mass which seemed widest and heaviest where he was close to the floor, and his orderless shoulders and sloping brow gave weight to the illusion that he could never be less than solidly upright like an anvil. He greeted her with words Humphrey did not understand and when she kissed his shaven head Humphrey momentarily felt something he would have described as apprehension rather than resentment. That man once was, she said later, a Sumo wrestler of national fame.

The bar-room was empty, except for a liveried attendant who poured their free champagne into fine tulip goblets and seemed pleased to see her. On the bar-top, open cedar boxes offered free Havana cigars and cigarettes from Britain, France, America, Morocco and Japan. The Japanese cigarettes were labelled Hope. Humphrey remembered that it had cost them nothing at the door, and, as they walked toward the crowded gambling rooms, she told him the costs were built into the house percentages.

She led him through. Short of the archway, it was noisy and difficult to make out individual sounds. Then, there was the roaring of conversation, clatter from roulette wheels, the irregular bouncing of dice, a fluttering of stiff cards, and, from the half-opened doorways of other rooms, the clacking of mah-jong. Spectators crowded three deep behind the gamblers at tables he could not see, and he guessed slowly that perhaps a third of the crowd was not Japanese.

A group of Indian women in saris moved out of his way. Their husbands wore western evening dress. One seemed about to greet her but Anita looked quickly away. Silly, she smiled, with his wife. Humphrey caught fragments of a conversation in French from three smartly dressed Asian men who were so tiny they had trouble pushing through the crush. Anita thought they were part of a diplomatic group recently exiled from Cambodia. He heard accents in English from America and Britain. At the craps table, Anita began to explain the game to him, but he stopped her because he could not grasp it quickly enough. The drunken and imponderable bouncing of the dice made him nervous and he moved away. All the house-dealers and croupiers he could see were women. From the head of a card table, a Chinese girl in a straight dress the sweetly glittering colour of angelica smiled as Anita waved to her. It seemed to be the only genuine gesture of pleasure he had seen since he entered. For six months, Anita told him, she had worked on the circuit: Macao, Las Vegas, Monaco, where a girl with a quick brain and a taut figure, she said, can make money like nowhere else. Humphrey had heard of it, expensively coiffured and preciously gowned women working at vingt-et-un, poker, black jack, and as croupiers at the long tables, where, he could see them here, the losers drink harder and billow cigar smoke to screen the amusement of the careless rich, and winners watch the wheel as their spinning eyes begin to glitter with the first lights of understanding and their hearts race to count the priceless intervals they have now begun to discover. The smoke stung his eyes. People moved from table to table, pushing through the crowd rudely and with a deep and fearful irritation. The only sounds of laughter he could hear were rueful, the vexed and contrary chords of disappointment. I do not like this, he said. The noises and the movements of the room were whirlpools of dread and hopelessness that unsteadied him. For the first time she took his hand. They like you to spend money at the tables, she said, but I can say I'm not feeling well. He saw the time was nearly two o'clock.

In the night-club, they were led to their table in darkness as the floor-show was about to begin. The curtain rose to a girl in a white and pleated nightgown, singing, evidently, from a book of songs she illuminated by a candle held in her hand. The effect was sweet and saddening.

Humphrey and Mimi were childless; Mimi's second miscarriage, her gynaecologist had told them with the morose jollity he used to lighten the boredom of repetition, extinguished the flame necessary to the conception of a life and no amount of stoking would fire it. They were unhappy for many months, until their heightened interest in other families discovered, not the songs-without-words of love and sacrifice, but parental groans of diminishing humour and growing penury, followed always by childish screams of greed and disappointment. It was a wonder to them that they had not seen it before. Both developed a dislike of children and an inability to bear childish games or the irritation of wandering interrogations for more than a few minutes at a time. Only during the safety of organised performances did Humphrey feel paternal longings, and, alongside parents and uncles and grandmothers, his eyes misted or his breast trembled a little at the choral obedience of precocious voices during church fests or in the cold schoolhalls of their friends' children.

A night-club was not where he would have expected it, but it seemed to Humphrey that this girl's voice had a clarity he had not heard before. Although the words were Japanese, the melodies were of Evensong and Christmastide. She sang with that slender tone singers manage to hold only during their teens. With the first song her body wavered in the light with the grace of a flame. In the next, she seemed to lose the delicate shape of its rhythm and Humphrey was annoyed by the harsh beginning of laughter in the audience. It was premature and unfair. Perhaps the Japanese who watched her did not understand the fragile and nostalgic simplicities which made these melodies delicious to the ear of the cultured westerner. They were light sounds, begun in the centuries of the lute and the dulcimer, carried by a single voice into the flower-gardens and along the corridors of feudal castles, or by many voices through Cathedrals whose old stone reflected its sparse geometry faithfully. Perhaps only Humphrey and this young Japanese singer understood that these melodies were cousin to the foundations of an entire European musical heritage. But laughter grew at the opening of her third song; it was loud and unashamed; something had happened to her delivery of the words that he did not understand and the gestures she made with her hips and shoulders were sometimes fitful and involuntary. Her fingers plucked at the bodice of her night-dress, and slid, immeasurably slowly, over the slim curve of her abdomen. To her timing of the song, she felt for the texture of her body.

Only when she began to lift the hem of her gown did Humphrey know he was watching a sex-show. That slight and innocent girl blew on the candle with an increasingly throaty and humid voice, and Humphrey closed his eyes. He heard the song come from her in small and wanton cries. As her panting quickened, cadences of her audience's laughter rolled in his ears. When the last applause had died, and the only sound he could hear was that of the dance-band, Humphrey looked up. The footlights were bright and stage attendants moved scenery for the next act. Well, Anita asked him, isn't she great? Humphrey's voice was uneven and the tears in his eyes were bitter. Terrific, he said.

His lustfulness was still deflated. His need for adventure was empty. Although he was tired, he thought it had nothing to do with the late hour. Instead of the excitement of a forbidden and clandestine world, she had shown him merely fragments of decay that made him apprehensive and wary. He had no wish to aspire to it. Under the velvet red of a bar lamp he had squinted at photographs of her and her younger sister; her early life was so like Mimi's; they were taken, she told him, east of Seattle, where her father owned a country property. He was a physician in city practice and they commuted weekends. On the backs of the photographs were written the names Helen and Jennifer. Her hair did not, then, have the cagey dross of an ash-blond, but the cadmium tints of summer swimming-pools, of horseback riding on crisp mornings, and of skiing the squeaking powders of fresh snowfalls. She had spent, she had said, a fresher year at high-school, taken credits in geography and biology to please her father, and made the basketball team. Her face was not then known to doormen and card-sharps, or her body to the businessmen of thirty countries. She did not then have to turn away from the greeting of dressy diplomats and introduce paying customers to bars, gambling houses and night-clubs.

Sitting in a profane and prodigal night-club next to a young and inexplicable whore was not where he wanted to be. He felt a fondness for the banal and lustreless dinner-tables of his friends and for the comfort of his own rooms and wardrobes, his office and his club. Before the lights darkened again for the next act he left the table, to find the toilet, he told her, paid on his way out, and took a cab back to his hotel.

It is ten o'clock before he wakes in the morning. His window-pane dribbles with rain but the certainty that his homecoming is less than two days – less than a day, flying time – away, gives him a sense of liberation and relief. His flight is at two. He orders a large breakfast that will save him also from an airport lunch, and he showers before it arrives. He has seldom felt so fit. He picks up the telephone and

153

dials the international operator. He will send a cable home. Arriving
Friday, she will read, After Midday.

It has occurred to him that he and Mimi should take a holiday.

Although that is all years ago now, Humphrey remembers his whore
from time to time. Always without nostalgia; rather, with slow and
furrowed amusement. He seldom takes a chair at Mimi's card parties,
and then only when pressed to make up a fourth, but sometimes the
noises of dice and roulette come to him, and Mimi is surprised that
her habitual underbidding makes him smile contentedly at her. They
now take vacations twice yearly, generally once at the coast with the
Sullivans, where they barbecue fillets of steak and lamb chops in
rosemary on the beach when the summer evenings are warmest,
telling of other friends and of other vacations to the coral beaches of
Fiji and the restaurants of Noumea and the fiords of New Zealand,
and Mimi interrupts the stories Humphrey has just begun, of the
gambling houses and night-clubs, as he puts it, of the orient, and
their friends will later remark that her sharp primness about those
things never seems to irk him.

More about Penguins and Pelicans

Other Australian fiction available in Penguin

Dirty Friends
Morris Lurie

In Tangier a lonely poet confronts the ugliest truth . . . in Greece a millionaire makes a dazzling escape . . . in Yugoslavia a marriage falters . . . in Melbourne a friendship shows its other face . . .

Wherever he is (Switzerland, New York), whomever he addresses (a fancy mistress, a wry Jewish uncle), Morris Lurie displays that uncanny mixture of humour and compassion which has won him an international audience.

'Reading Morris Lurie's stories . . . is like having a brilliant, funny friend. It's not that he's always good for a laugh, which he is, but also that he's a help when the going gets tough. He faces sadness, even tragedy with spirit.' Bruce Grant, *Australian Book Review*

'Lurie has that kind of acute appreciation of social farce that tots up to a real observation of the styles of the culture.' Malcolm Bradbury, *Guardian*

'a real feeling of civilized man's unease in an urban environment where nobody seems to fit . . . good serious entertainment.' R. G. C. Price, *Punch*

Voss
Patrick White

The plot of this novel is of epic simplicity: in 1845 Voss
sets out with a small band to cross the Australian
continent for the first time. The tragic story of their
terrible journey and its inevitable end is told with
imaginative understanding.

The figure of Voss takes on superhuman proportions,
until he appears to those around him as both deliverer
and destroyer. His relationship with Laura Trevelyan is
the central personal theme of the story.

The true record of Ludwig Leichhardt, who dies in the
Australian desert in 1848, suggested *Voss* to the author.

'A work of genius . . . *Voss* has an epic quality, the ageless
sense of the power and pride of man battling with his
condition' – John Davenport in the *Observer*

'In size, intention and achievement, *Voss* is the work of a
man for whom Tolstoy is the only fitting rival' –
Penelope Mortimer in the *Sunday Times*

The Twyborn Affair
Patrick White

In a crumbling villa in the south of France,
Eudoxia loves her ageing, obsessive Greek, Angelos.

After the Great War, Eddie comes home to an uneasy
reunion with his parents in Australia, then flees to the
outback.

In London, Eadith presides as the flamboyant madam of
an exclusive brothel, until the conflagration of another
war closes in.

Yet none of them can escape the torment of their
confused passions and identity.

'Wonderfully entertaining, varied and satisfying' – Angus
Wilson in the *Observer*

'Impressive in its conception, astonishing in its concrete-
ness, sharp in its sardonic social discriminations . . .'
William Walsh in the *Times Literary Supplement*

The Transit of Venus
Shirley Hazzard

The Transit of Venus is a novel of place: Sydney, London,
New York, Stockholm; of time: from the fifties to the
eighties; and above all, of destiny: of the two beautiful,
orphaned sisters, Caro and Grace Bell, and the men in
their lives.

'a great novel of passion and ambition, success and failure,
written with elegance and wit and magnificently
structured . . . a fine celebration of passion and the
perennial sexual battle . . . a work of warmth, wit and
very great humour' *Australian Book Review*

'Shirley Hazzard's writing is sumptuous' *The Times*
(London)

'This engrossing, masterly novel . . . combines the
satisfaction of a family saga . . . with a highly structured
plot reminiscent of Greek tragedy, with its sense of doom
and its implied acceptance of larger patterns beyond an
individual's fate' *New York Times Book Review*

'Among Hazzard's many strengths as a novelist, none is
more dazzling than her ability to display the inner world
of her characters in a few lines of lucid, supple, periodic
prose' *Time*